A Hummingbird Dance

Praise for *The Lucky Elephant Restaurant,* the second installment of the Detective Lane Series and winner of the 2007 Lambda Literary Award for Gay Mystery

"Lane and Harper are fine characters who deserve a series."
The Globe and Mail

"Ryan has penned a haunting, psychological drama of the first order."
Edmonton Journal

"Watching Lane and Harper unpeel the layers of this particular onion is an amazing experience."
The Star Phoenix

"Ryan balances suspense with humour, creating books that are, quite simply, a great read."
Aloft Magazine

"The second Detective Lane mystery is even better than the first, and that's saying a lot."
Drewey Wayne Gunn, author of *The Gale Male Sleuth in Print and Film*

"Ryan breaks down all forms of stereotypes including those surrounding disability, sexual orientation, race and religion. He doesn't give the reader any opportunity to disassociate from the novel's message, since he sets it all right here in Calgary. What emerges at the core is a message of respect toward all people."
BeatRoute Magazine

A Hummingbird Dance

Garry Ryan

NeWest Press

Copyright ©
Garry Ryan 2008

Library and Archives Canada Cataloguing in Publication

Ryan, Garry, 1953–
A hummingbird dance / Garry Ryan.
ISBN 978-1-897126-31-8
I. Title.
PS8635.Y354H84 2008   C813'.6   C2008-902312-9

Editor for the Board: Douglas Barbour
Cover and interior design: Natalie Olsen
Cover photo: Garry Ryan
Author photo: Karma Ryan

NeWest Press acknowledges the support of the Canada Council for the Arts, the Alberta Foundation for the Arts, and the Edmonton Arts Council for our publishing program. We also acknowledge the financial support of the Government of Canada through the Book Publishing Industry Development Program (BPIDP).

201-8540-109 Street
Edmonton, Alberta T6G 1E6
(780) 432-9427

NeWest Press   newestpress.com

No bison were harmed in the making of this book.
We are committed to protecting the environment and to the responsible use of natural resources. This book is printed on 100% recycled, ancient forest-friendly paper.

1 2 3 4 5 11 10 09 08   printed and bound in Canada

For Mike, Denise, Nick, Luke, and Indiana.

ch*a*pter 1

"Christine called."

Arthur was sitting in a lawn chair with a glass of lemonade atop his generous belly. He still wore dirt-stained gloves, and the knees of his grey sweatpants were black.

Lane found himself unable to speak. His mind turned into a shovel, digging and turning over memories just as he'd spent yesterday turning over the soil in the flower beds. He thought, *I had it under control; I could handle it by not thinking about it. Now, just mention her name, and I'm back where it all started.* "The flowers look great." He looked around the yard at the annuals and peren- nials Arthur had planted today for their first summer in this house. It looked like a Monet. All of those im- possibly bright waves of colour running up against and into one another.

"Did you hear me? I said Christine called." Arthur glared at Lane.

"I heard you." Lane was already exhausted with memories of her. He thought about what she looked like and realized that today he probably wouldn't recognize her if he bumped into her on the street.

"She wouldn't leave a message. She did say that she'll call back tonight at ten. It's just enough time." Arthur drained the last of the lemonade and took off his gloves.

"Enough time?" Lane thought, *Things should start to get easier now with this family. We've had more than enough time since it all happened.*

"We have to pick up Matt at the bus station in thirty minutes." Arthur took a closer look at Lane.

"He planned on being gone for at least a week. It's only been two days." Lane reached into his pocket for car keys.

Arthur walked over and put a hand on Lane's shoulder. "I'll drive. Matt left a message. He sounded pretty upset. He asked us to pick him up."

Lane looked up at Arthur.

"Christine's call has really shaken you." Arthur lead the way along the deck and out the gate to the driveway. He put his palm on Lane's cheek. "This is how I felt when Matt arrived with no warning, and no time to prepare myself."

Automatically, Lane looked around to see if any of the neighbours had witnessed the public display of affection. "What did she say?"

Arthur opened the Jeep's passenger door, then walked around the front.

Lane got in and shut his door.

Arthur got in behind the wheel. "Put your seat belt on."

Lane heard the sound of waves sifting their frothy way up a beach. His mind wandered in and out of focus. His hand guided the the seat belt automatically into the lock. "What did she say, exactly?" He looked at the deck and the honeysuckle growing up the chain link.

Arthur started the engine. "She said, 'This is Christine. Is Lane there?' I explained you were at work and she said, 'I'll call back tonight at ten.' It's a good thing we kept the same phone number."

"No indication of where she was calling from?"

"None." Arthur eased the Jeep out of the driveway. "I've been trying to remember how old she is."

"Seventeen." Lane's cellphone rang. He reached instinctively into his sports-coat pocket. "Hello."

"Lane? It's Harper. We've got a missing cowboy. You and I've been assigned to it. I'll call you later when I've got more of the details." Harper hung up.

Lane closed his phone.

When they reached the Greyhound bus station on Ninth Avenue, he tried to recall how they got there.

"You look awful," Matt said to Lane. Their nephew threw his bag into the back of the Jeep and crawled into the rear seat.

Arthur looked at Lane, nodding in agreement with Matt's diagnosis.

Lane watched the boy closely. His black hair was cut short. His chin was peppered with acne and he'd removed his earring. There were dark circles under his red-rimmed eyes.

Arthur and Lane climbed in. They waited, in silent agreement, for Matt to speak.

It was quiet for the first eleven minutes as they left downtown and drove north, then west toward the mountains.

"Hungry?" Arthur asked.

"Nope." Matt looked out the side window.

"Want to talk?" Arthur asked.

"Nope." Matt continued to look away.

They drove up Sarcee Trail in silence. When they got home, Matt grabbed his bag out of the back. "I'm going to bed." His gently lurching CP gait seemed more pronounced as he made his way inside and downstairs to his bedroom.

"What do you think happened?" Arthur opened the door and stepped inside.

"I don't know." Lane checked the phone to see if there were any messages.

"Should we go and talk with him?" Arthur paced the kitchen.

"Let him sleep. It looks like he needs the rest. Maybe he'll feel like talking in the morning." Lane looked at the clock on the stove. It read eight o'clock.

"She said she'd call at ten," Arthur said.

"I know."

Lane's cellphone rang at twenty after ten. He flipped it open. "Hello."

"It's me," Harper said. "Shhhhh."

"What?"

"Sorry, just got Jessica to sleep."

"You're holding her now?" Lane asked.

"Yep. It's crazy, but if I walk and talk she falls asleep. The moment I stop talking or walking, she starts crying again. She's already got me tied around her little finger."

"Kids." Lane looked at the clock and thought about Christine not calling, Matt not talking, and Harper's infant daughter, who had changed the logical, outspoken detective into a proud daddy with her voice recorded on his pocket computer.

"Tell me about it. Anyway, I found out some more about our missing person. Name's Ryan Dudley. Went out for a ride on his horse. The horse came back without him. Sounds like a real cliché, eh? Same address as Tyler McNally who disappeared last year. Both disappeared on June thirtieth. Both went to the same high school."

"How come we were assigned this one? I'm assuming the victims live in the country."

"They live near T'suu Tina. You know, the reserve. The land north of there was recently annexed by the city, so it's our case." Harper started making cooing sounds to soothe his daughter.

"The date is probably significant." Lane looked at Arthur, sleeping and snoring on the couch.

"I'll check that out tomorrow. The chief called me. She thinks there's gonna be a lot of pressure to have this one solved quickly. Ryan was a rodeo competitor. The Stampede's only a couple of weeks away. You know how twitchy everyone downtown gets about Stampede attendance. On top of that there's some noise about a land claim. This one could get real messy."

So, what else is new, Lane thought. His doorbell rang. Arthur stopped snoring but did not wake.

"See you in the morning at the gym." Harper hung up.

Lane closed his phone. The doorbell rang again. He walked to the front door, checked the peephole. A young woman with black hair and a face distorted by the fisheye lens stared back at him.

Lane opened the inside door. She studied him through the glass of the screen door.

He opened the outside door with his right hand. Lane looked at the young woman's face and felt like his heart was running a marathon. The girl had close-cropped black hair, a black, short-cut jacket, pink skirt, white socks and white shoes. Lane thought she looked like an impressionist's version of a twenty-first century rebellious female who had recently moved to the city from Avonlea.

"What happened to your old house?" the girl asked.

"That's a long story." Lane looked closer at the face. There was a hint of Africa on her skin. Then he looked at the garbage bag leaning up against her leg. There were light green marks on the bag where the dark green plastic had been stretched beyond capacity.

"The old place is a long way from here. I had to check the most recent return addresses on your letters." She glanced at the shoe box under her left arm. "A bus driver told me how to get here. Thanks for the money, by the way. I checked. You never missed a birthday or Christmas. I would have been lost without the money."

"Christine?" Lane's throat was so constricted he almost choked on her name.

"Uncle Lane, you remembered. I was afraid you wouldn't." She moved closer to hug him around the chest with her free arm.

Lane wrapped his left arm around her shoulders. She smelled of the country.

The garbage bag leaned over and spilled half of its t-shirts, underpants, and a brand new sports brassiere that rolled down the steps.

"Who's there?" Arthur's voice was full of sleep.

"My friend's mom warned me I was going to be excommunicated." Christine sat at the kitchen table, eating salad and fanning five slender fingers in front of her mouth each time she talked.

Lane and Arthur sat on either side of her.

"How come?" Arthur's eyes were drooping. He nodded before raising his head back up.

"How come she warned me?" Christine asked.

"How come you were going to be excommunicated?" Arthur leaned his chin on his fist.

Christine dropped her fork and rubbed her scalp. The hair was a uniform length of less than two centimetres. "I shaved my head."

"That's it?" Lane asked.

"Well, the day before that I asked Mr. Whitemore if it was true he told a reporter that girls of fourteen and fifteen weren't married off to older men in Paradise." Christine looked at one and then the other, waiting for a response.

"I'm not sure I follow," Arthur said.

"Paradise practices plural marriage. There was a documentary on TV. My cousin told me about it." Christine shovelled more salad into her mouth.

"Oh." Arthur leaned back.

"Was it true?" Lane asked.

"About the girls?" Christine asked from behind her fingers.

Lane nodded.

"One of my friends was married off at fourteen and another at fifteen. Whitemore said on the TV show that girls weren't married until they were at least eighteen."

"And?" Lane waited for more. He thought, *How did she end up in Paradise?*

"He lied." Christine shrugged. "He told us to tell the truth and he lied."

"How, exactly did you get away?" Lane asked.

"I was packed and ready when the confusion started." Christine looked out the window.

Lane waited.

"Well my friend's mom didn't want her fourteen-year-old daughter married off to a sixty-year-old man from Utah, so she jammed the cupboards in her house full of kindling, made sure everyone was outside, then set fire to the place. While everyone else in Paradise was trying to put out the fire, she left with her daughter. I walked in the other direction."

MONDAY, JULY 1

ch*a*pter 2

Harper and Lane put equipment bags in the trunk of their unmarked Chevrolet.

"So this kid is your niece, you haven't seen her in more than ten years, and she's from Paradise?" Harper eased his football player's frame into the driver's seat.

"And, I'm her godfather." Lane opened the passenger door.

"You know about Paradise?" Harper started the engine.

He looks a little tired this morning, Lane thought. "Jessica okay?"

"She was up in the night. Erinn's beat. Glenn could sleep through a hurricane. So, I was up walking Jessica for a couple of hours 'til she finally nodded off. I woke up on the couch with her drooling on my chest." Looking over at Lane, Harper said, "Don't change the subject."

"Okay, what do *you* know about Paradise?" Lane put his seat belt on.

"Fundamentalist polygamist group near the US border. There are other polygamist communities in Utah, Arizona, and Texas. The communities trade young women back and forth to marry older men." Harper backed out before shifting into drive and making for Crowchild Trail. "The older guys often kick the teen-aged boys out because of the competition for females. Want to know more?"

Lane shook his head. *Too much information,* he thought. "What about the cowboy who disappeared?" *How did my sister end up in Paradise?*

"The story of the missing cowboy is getting more interesting by the hour," Harper said.

"How's that?"

"I think I've found a pattern. Wanna check it out?" Harper accelerated.

Aidan put on a black ball cap. The fingers of her right hand tucked a wayward strand of blonde hair behind her ear. She carefully packed away the four heads of cowboy marionettes sitting in pairs in the crew cab of a pickup she'd built. Its front license plate was stamped with *Republic of Alberta*. She placed the cowboys in a metre-long case designed to fold out into one section of the set. In each of the other felt-lined maple cases, the marionettes hung by hooks so their strings wouldn't become tangled.

One male and one female marionette sat nearby. The female had blonde hair and blue eyes. Her face was large, out of proportion to her body. She wore black. The male's face was as large, with dark hair and large brown eyes. He wore a fluorescent pink shirt, pride-orange pants, royal-blue socks, and jacaranda-purple shoes.

Aidan picked up the marionettes by the strings so they faced one another. She began to speak in two voices. The first was decidedly sarcastic and male. The second was hers.

"You know this isn't my real voice. I won't speak. Lots of hearing people wanted me to speak, then tried to correct me when it came out different from what they expected. Some even laughed at me." Alex, the male, placed his hands on his hips.

"I know, I know. But this is a show. Most of the audience is hearing. They need to listen to your story. Don't worry, if anyone in the audience is deaf, I'll have an interpreter to sign," Aidan, the female marionette, said.

"You're really going to do this?" Alex held out his right hand.

"Yes." She dropped her gaze.

"You know what will happen, don't you?" He shook his head. "I mean, I can't stop you, you're the puppeteer. But this will probably get messy. And you're a woman. Things always get messier for women. I tried to tell you what it was like before I died."

"That's why we're opening at the rodeo. I need to see the faces of that audience, how they react to what we have to say about what happened. Then I'll know."

"What? What will you know?" he asked.

"If they understand what it is we're trying to say about what happened to you. How those four guys got away with what they did to you. How the Premier talked about you as if your life didn't count for much."

Alex shook his head. "And don't forget what this has done to you."

Harper aimed the Chev down a straight section of the two-lane highway on the west side of the city. "Two years ago, a seventeen-year-old named Alexander Starchild was killed along this road."

Lane looked left and right, where a mix of evergreen and poplar trees grew behind a barbed-wire fence. To the west the mountains were white-tipped and seemed magnified, closer somehow.

"He was hit while trying to hitchhike into the city. He and a friend were going to a movie. The friend saw the hit and run pickup truck. She didn't get the rear license plate. Apparently the front plate had *Republic of Alberta* on it. The witness said there were four cowboys inside. One opened the passenger door and the driver steered right over onto the shoulder. Alexander was hit by the door and killed instantly. The mirror hit him in the back of the head. It happened on June thirtieth, two years ago," Harper said.

"No leads on the truck?" Lane asked.

"None. Then these two guys disappear a year apart. They lived on an acreage only a few kilometres from where Alex Starchild lived." Harper eased his foot off the accelerator. "That's way too many coincidences."

"I'll have to check with Lisa and find out what the RCMP have on the case." Lane looked at the map on his knees. "Should be the next left."

Harper flicked the left turn signal, braked, and turned on to the side road. Gravel spattered and rattled against the underside of the car. Lane noticed that the bottom of the ditch was still shiny with water from the last rain.

They travelled five more kilometres south. A cloud of dust rolled out in a horizontal column, following them even after they hit the paved driveway. The ranch-style house was roofed with red tiles, sided in brick, and attached to a four-car garage. Behind the house was a pasture of hay. Lane could see it was waiting for its first cut. To the south, a silver Quonset hut sat at one end of a corral.

Harper parked next to a black 4×4 pickup truck. Lane got out of the car and adjusted his Glock pistol in its hip holster. There was barking around the back of the house. Lane looked across the roof of the car at Harper. They stepped back into the car as a German shepherd rounded the corner. It was all teeth and rage. The dog put its paws on Lane's door and growled.

"Get down Rosco! Down!" A man walked around the side of the house and grabbed the dog by its collar. The man was dressed in new, skin-tight blue jeans, a black shirt open at the collar, and a black felt hat pulled low so his eyes were hidden in shade. The toes of his his boots were tipped with silver. A belt buckle the size of a dessert plate polished off the look.

"Who are you guys?"

Lane thought, *This one would be wearing jackboots and a brown shirt given the right political climate.*

Harper and Lane held up their IDs.

"Oh." The man frowned. "It's okay, come out. It's safe." He backed away, dragging the dog with him. "You here about Duds?"

Harper got out. "Ryan Dudley?"

Lane got out, but left his door open. "You called him Duds?"

"That's right."

Lane decided that a change in approach was required. "I'm Detective Lane."

"You?" The man looked at Harper.

"Detective Harper. You?"

"Blake. Blake Rogers." He tipped his hat back.

"We're here to discuss Mr. Dudley's disappearance," Lane said.

"He left around eight in the morning, yesterday. His horse came back about four hours later. He liked to ride along the river. We looked for him there, but found nothing." Blake lifted his hat, revealing close-cut black hair.

"Who's we?" Lane asked.

"Me and Skip." Blake glanced at the pickup.

"Skip?" Lane kept his eyes on Blake, observing his reactions.

Harper looked over his shoulder at the truck.

Blake smiled. "Skip Lombardi. He went into the city. Works there. He'll be back around six."

"May we see Mr. Dudley's horse and saddle?" Lane asked.

"He kept it at a stable down the road. They phoned when the horse came back without him." Blake kept a smile ready, like the round tin of chewing tobacco in his back pocket.

Lane pulled out a card. "When Mr. Lombardi gets back, give me a call. We need to meet with him as well." He handed the card to Blake.

"Sure thing." Blake put the card in his shirt pocket.

"How would you describe Mr. Dudley's behaviour in the last few days? Anything unusual?" Harper asked.

It's interesting that Blake's smile gets wider when he looks at Harper, Lane thought.

"Same old Duds. Ornery one minute, laughin' the next. Nothin' unusual at all." Blake rubbed his free hand across the stubble on his chin.

"Which way is the stable?" Lane watched Blake carefully.

Blake said, "Back to the highway, then five klicks west. It's called Glencoe Stables. Just follow the signs." He continued to smile at Harper.

"Thank you." Lane climbed back into the Chev.

Blake shook Harper's hand. It took Harper a few seconds to free himself from the grip.

Rosco ran after them 'til their car passed the gate at the end of the driveway.

Three kilometres down the road, Lane said, "Did you notice?"

Harper looked at his partner. "Notice what?"

"He was coming on to you. Blake Rogers is gay," Lane said.

"You're jokin'." Harper looked sideways at Lane.

Lane smiled. "It's simply an observation."

Harper's face reddened. "What say we visit the Starchild place? It's on the way."

"Think we'll get more information there than at the

stables?" Lane asked. He thought about adding, "big boy," but decided against it.

"The dates are bothering me. It can't be a coincidence that all three occurred on June thirtieth." Harper pulled a map out and handed it to Lane. "The route is highlighted in blue."

They found the Starchild home in twenty minutes. It was about one hundred metres off the main gravel road running east and west alongside the T'suu Tina Nation. Trees lined the north and south sides of the house. The fifteen-metre evergreens provided a break from winter winds. A column of grey smoke climbed straight up into the windless sky. Harper maneuvered the Chev along the ridges of a mud-rutted dirt road running between the house and the evergreens. They moved around the back of the faded blue bungalow.

"What's that?" Harper asked.

"Not sure." Lane looked at a domed, tent-like structure set up in front of a Quonset hut. A man dressed in khaki bib overalls, green shirt, khaki-coloured cowboy hat, and six-gun holster tended a fire burned down to embers. Heat shimmered and distorted the structures behind it. The man turned to watch the detectives as they stopped and got out of the car.

Harper spoke first. "We're looking for …"

"Me," a woman said. She stepped out of the open door of the Quonset. She wore a zippered sweater open in the front. Under that was a blue nightie reaching from her neck to her ankles. She wore a pair of white running shoes and more than half a century of winters on her face.

"I'm Detective Harper and this is—" Harper said.

"I know. You're the police. Come to ask about that

disappeared fella." The woman's voice was a combination of soft-spoken command and blunt honesty.

The man with the overalls and empty holster leaned on a pitch fork. He tipped back his cowboy hat, revealing an asymmetrical forehead with a ridge riding along the crown. The scar revealed itself as he lifted his hat to wipe the sweat from his brow with the inside of his elbow. He pulled the hat back down and tucked the string under his chin.

"This is Norm and I'm Eva Starchild. I'm Alex's grandmother. You're just in time for the sweat. Hope you brought shorts and towels. You can get changed in the back of the Quonset." Eva turned to the opening of the dome. She adjusted what looked like several blankets arranged carefully over a series of supports intersecting at the top and centre of the sweat lodge.

"We came to talk," Lane said.

Eva didn't turn around. "We're just about ready for the sweat. You can sit outside in the car and wait until we're done or you can come inside. Up to you. If you come inside, you'll want to change those clothes."

Harper looked at Lane.

Lane watched the old woman as she arranged an altar in front of the dome. He was sure she was smiling even though there was no indication of it on her face.

"Start the rocks," Eva said.

"You betcha." Norm used the pitchfork to pick a five kilogram rock out of the fire. He guided it inside the sweat lodge and dropped it into a hole in the centre.

Lane moved around to the trunk of the Chev.

Harper followed.

Lane opened the trunk lid.

"What do you think you're doing?" Harper pulled back his jacket, revealing his Glock. His fists rested on his hips.

Lane took his holster and pistol off. He checked the Glock's safety before setting it down gently on the floor of the trunk.

"I don't like it." Harper looked at the sweat lodge. "You have no idea what you're walking into."

"We're not going to learn much out here." Lane grabbed his black gym bag.

"I'll keep an eye out and call it in. I'm just not sure what to call it, exactly."

"Thanks." Lane made his way to the back of the Quonset, where he saw a table saw, mitre saw, router, various drills, sanders, and a couple of work tables. The place smelled of wood and stain. *A carpenter lives here,* he thought.

Harper watched two pickups arrive. One hit a dip in the road and its driver's side fender flapped like a chicken wing. There were four people sandwiched into each cab. The men got out. They wore sweatpants and T-shirts while the women wore sweaters and nighties.

One of the men looked at Norm and then at Harper. "Hey, Norm."

"Hey, Leo." Norm nodded at the men as they walked toward the sweat lodge. He tipped his hat to the women.

Eva crawled out of the lodge on hands and knees. "Just two more stones, Norm. Hey, everybody. Alex would appreciate this."

Lane walked out of the Quonset in bare feet, shorts and a T-shirt. He took in the scene and the new arrivals, who showed not a hint of surprise on their faces.

Eva said, "Time to smudge." She lit the end of what looked to Lane like a short piece of braided rope and set it in a bowl. He watched the others. One by one, they bent over the bowl and guided the smoke over their heads, bodies and arms. Then they crawled inside.

Lane inhaled the pleasant scent of the smoke while imitating their actions before ducking inside the womb of the sweat lodge. He was in the middle of the group of ten. He sat with his head close to the roof and his toes warmed by the heated rocks stacked in the hollow at the centre of the circle.

He watched as Eva crawled in and sat cross-legged next to a man who held a drum. Norm passed a five gallon pail of water in and closed the flaps over the opening. Lane was enveloped in total darkness. He felt sweat running down from the edge of his hairline. He pulled his T-shirt off and used it to wipe sweat from his eyes. His lungs filled with moist air as water was poured onto the rocks. The steam was scented with tobacco and tasted sharp on the tongue.

"So, you're a cop?" Norm sat in a lawn chair two metres from the fire pit. He stretched his legs out, crossed one cowboy boot over the other and interlocked his fingers across his belly.

"Yes." Harper pulled up a vacant chair. He moved back as the heat from the embers cooked his face and hands. "How long will they be in there?"

"Depends," Norm said.

"On what?"

"If your friend can last four rounds or not." Norm looked at Harper and smiled.

Harper heard the sound of a drum coming from inside the sweat lodge. He looked around the yard and spotted a row of six evergreen trees running along the southern edge of the property.

"Alex started plantin' those six years ago. Planted a new one the beginning of every summer. Each year he picked out a tree that was six feet tall and watched it grow. Used to water each one twice a week. Now I do the waterin' and the plantin'."

Harper looked closely at the trees as they went from tallest to shortest. The most recent one was staked and tied to keep the north and west winds from blowing it over. On this side of the trees, honeysuckle formed a white and red foreground. Something hovered in front of a red flower.

"What's that?" Harper pointed.

Norm looked right. "You mean the hummer?"

"Hummer?"

"Hummingbird. Only place I know 'round here where hummers stay all summer." Norm pointed at the trees. "Planted that one just a couple of days ago." He pointed at his chest with a purple-bruised fingernail.

"How come the next to last tree isn't the same height?" Harper asked.

Norm looked at the tree. It stood between eight and nine feet tall. The tips of the branches were a brighter shade of green where new growth added to the tree's girth and height. "Must be the water. Artesian."

The back screen door of Eva's house opened with a creak. Both men turned.

A young woman backed out of the door carrying a wooden case. She wore white coveralls, tan work boots and a red silk shirt. Her blonde hair was tucked under a black ball cap.

"Need a hand, Aidan?" Norm was on his feet and moving toward the house.

Harper followed. As he watched her carry the case, he thought, *I've never seen anyone look so elegant in work clothes*. He watched her move with the grace and poise of an athlete.

"Aidan used to be in the ballet." Norm took the case from her.

Harper opened the tailgate of a nearby pickup. He grabbed one end of the case and helped Norm slide it into the back of the truck. Harper noted that the truck box was coated with a plastic liner and thick blankets were carefully laid out on the bed to protect the finish of the wood.

"Careful," Norm said, "These are Aidan's mary ... marion ..."

"Marionettes," Aidan said.

Norm talked as they worked. "Aidan talks to Alex now. At first I thought she was talkin' to a ghost, but she says it's just a way to keep him alive in her mind. And she says it's art. Some people just don't understand art, I guess."

Aidan glared at Norm. His mouth closed.

Harper helped carry the next four cases to the truck. He saw that each was made of maple, engraved with a stylized, long-beaked bird and finished with a clear stain. "These are beautiful."

"Aidan made 'em." Norm looked at Aidan. "Sometimes when I watch her talk, I think that Alex is alive. It's like magic. I just love watchin' the mary …"

"Marionettes," Aidan said.

Norm scratched his head. "Can never remember that word. Too long for me."

They gingerly loaded the last box.

"How come you're not in there, Aidan?" Norm nodded in the direction of the sweat lodge.

"A cop's in there." Aidan waited for Harper's reaction.

Norm turned to Harper. "Aidan hates cops. Don't mind 'em myself. At least you seem like a nice fella."

Harper studied Aidan. She weighed maybe a hundred and twenty pounds, yet there was something in the way she looked back at him that said she was someone who was ready to fight if need be. She was a tiger.

Norm adopted a deeper, more official tone. "She got arrested for protesting downtown 'cause the Premier called Alex the victim of the week. Then a city cop said, 'Why didn't the dumb wagon burner just get out of the way?' Aidan got arrested 'cause she punched the cop in the mouth."

Aidan stared Harper down.

"Cop's name was Stockwell. Aidan just calls 'im The Asshole," Norm said.

"Then we agree." Harper smiled.

"On what?" Aidan looked directly at Harper.

"Stockwell's middle name." Harper thought, *Oh shit, did I actually say that?* For an instant it looked like Aidan might be about to smile.

She glared at Harper. "Don't patronize me."

"Just telling you what I think." Harper stared back at her with frank interest.

"The Asshole pushed my face down on to the ground and broke my nose. He put his knee in my back and cracked a rib." Aidan stared back.

"I understand the charges against you were dropped." Harper closed the pickup's tailgate.

"Yes, but he's still a cop."

"And he's still an asshole." Harper backed away from the truck.

"Thanks for helping with my stuff." Aidan walked to the cab of the truck, got in, started up, and drove away.

"She and Alex were friends at school. She learned sign language so they could talk. She was with 'im when he was killed. He never heard the truck comin'. Born deaf. That's why he never got out of the way. She took it the hardest. At least that's what people say. Aidan and Alex were like brother and sister. Now she talks to Alex the mary ..."

"Marionette." Harper followed Norm back to his lawn chair where heat still made the air shiver above the embers.

"So, she saw who ran Alex down." Harper sat down next to Norm.

"Yep. Come on. I need some help with the barbecue." Norm walked into the Quonset and pulled out a barbecue with one of its two wheels missing. Harper grabbed the other end and helped carry it outside. Norm used a block of wood to level the barbecue before starting it up.

"What was Alex like?" Harper watched as Norm lit the barbecue with a match.

"Trickster. Used to play jokes on people. Never played no jokes on me." Norm closed the lid when the fuel ignited.

"Trickster?" Harper studied the deliberate way Norm moved.

"You never heard of the Trickster? Eva tells me stories all the time. Funny stories about how Trickster is smarter than everyone else." Norm sat down. "Let it heat up for a minute."

Harper sat down. *This is like talking with a kid,* he thought. "You live with Eva?"

"Nope. Got my own place." Norm reached into the cooler, got a can of Pepsi for himself and handed one to Harper.

"Thanks." Harper opened the can and took a sip. "What do you do?"

"Hired hand." Norm put his pop on the ground. He held his callused hands out. "Got good strong hands."

"In the winter?"

"Got a TV." Norm stood up. "You watch the news?"

"I try not to." Harper studied Norm who looked intently back.

"You know about the problems with gangs?" Norm tipped his hat back.

"Yes." Harper thought, *I wonder where this is going?*

"Lotta people around here worried about gangs. The city just keeps pushing closer." Norm looked at the fire and frowned.

"You worried?" Harper watched the way Norm's forehead furrowed when he was thinking.

Norm nodded. "Them biker gangs. Saw them on the news. They buy a place out in the country, then trouble starts. Ain't right." Norm pointed with his index finger. "Around here we keep an eye out for trouble. Gotta keep an eye out for guys like that."

"Any bikers out here?"

Norm shook his head as he considered the question. "Not yet. There's just a group of young fellas." Norm pointed in the general direction of the mountains. "Caused some trouble a while back."

Harper waited for Norm to continue. When he didn't, Harper asked, "Who?"

"Not sayin'. Time to get the meat started. Wanna help?"

"What kind of policeman are you?" Eva sat with a plate of barbecued buffalo ribs, pasta salad, and home-baked bread on her lap. Her black, braided hair hung off either shoulder, framing her round face.

Lane had just taken a sip of water, intent on replacing the moisture he'd sweated out. He choked. Harper patted his back.

Lane looked around the circle of people in lawn chairs. No one laughed or smiled at his predicament. They were, he could tell, waiting for an answer.

"You okay?" Harper asked.

Lane nodded. His senses were filled with what had happened inside the sweat lodge. *There are no words to explain what happened in there,* he thought.

People ate quietly, expectantly.

Harper looked at the buffalo ribs on his paper plate, then at the plastic fork and knife in his hands.

He put the utensils down and picked up the meat with his fingers.

"I look for missing people," Lane said.

"So you're lookin' for those missing cow ..." Eva hesitated intentionally, "... boys."

"That's right." Without thinking, he asked, "How come you're talking to me and wouldn't talk with the other officers?"

"They only talked *at* me. You started by listening to me and respecting the sweat lodge. This is Alex's sweat. It's the anniversary of his funeral." Eva sat without touching her food. "You knew it was his sweat?"

"No." Lane shook his head.

"After we eat, there is something for you to see," Eva said.

Lane watched the conversation turn to other matters. There was more and more laughter as Alex was remembered through the stories people told. While Norm sat next to Eva as if guarding her, others went to the tailgates of the pickups where the food was.

After she finished eating and was able to extricate herself from the various eddies of conversation in that river of talk, Eva stood and walked over to Lane. He was wiping his fingers on a paper napkin. "Come on," she said to Lane and Harper.

They followed her to the house. She had a rolling, brisk way of walking. The detectives had to hurry to catch up.

The back door opened into a kitchen with a maple table and eight oak chairs from different families and eras. Along one wall there were pictures of a dancer and others of frozen hummingbirds with their beaks into the white and red of honeysuckle. "Aidan took those pictures."

In the corner, a computer sat on a desk near the window. Eva sat down in front of it and tapped the mouse with her index finger. "Alex got this for me for Christmas a few years back. Wanted me to keep up on the powwows, news, and land claims. He was teaching me how to use it before he died." The screen resolved itself into the image of a dancer frozen in a swirl of reds, greens, and white. She pointed at the dancer. "Alex."

Lane and Harper stood on either side of Eva, looking over her shoulders. The room filled with the scent of smoke, sage, sweat, and tobacco. *It's not unpleasant,* Lane thought.

Eva used two fingers to type in her password. "Been getting one of these every couple of days." Eva clicked on an email message. In a couple of seconds it resolved itself into an image:

Hockey Star Disappears
Rodeo Rider Disappears
We know you're responsible and we're coming for you!

Harper pulled out his electronic agenda and began to enter information.

"When did you receive this email?" Lane asked.

"Couple days ago." Eva turned on the printer. "I'll make you a copy."

"Haven't seen that in a while." Harper drove with the window down.

Lane left his window up. He thought, *The smell of sage*

mixed with tobacco isn't bad, even when it's in the pores.

"I said …" Harper looked across at Lane.

"What do you mean?" Lane looked ahead.

"You're smiling, even though you're a little malodorous."

Lane's grin grew wider. "Where did 'malodorous' come from?"

"Glenn. Used it to describe Jessica after an especially nasty diaper. But then, at your house, kids usually arrive on the doorstep fully grown with garbage bags full of clothes. That's some system you've got!"

Lane shook his head. The thought of Jessica's diaper made him decide it was time to open his window. The wind felt fresh on his face. "Yes. What is that all about, anyway? How come the kids always arrive with garbage bags?"

"I'm surprised you missed that one. Glenn explained it to me. They're throwaway kids. For some reason, one or both of their parents have tossed them out like the trash. That's the way Glenn arrived at our house. Just him and the clothes on his back."

Lane thought for a moment. "It makes me wonder what happened to Alex's parents that he ended up living with his grandmother."

"Want me to check it out?" Harper asked.

"That and where the email came from. While you're doing that, I'll be checking up on our friend Blake. I'll call Lisa to find out what she knows."

"And, since we're on the topic, how about checkin' in at work? I can't cover for you forever. The new staff sergeant is starting to ask questions and I'm running out of excuses."

chapter 3

"I don't know what to do with these two." Arthur went to hug Lane, then backed away when he caught a whiff. "What have you been up to?"

"Maybe we'd better talk outside." Lane took his wine glass, went out the back door onto the deck. He sat down across from Arthur. The sun was low in the sky. The heat of the day was a lazy cat in their backyard.

"You smell like smoke." Arthur crossed his legs.

"Where are they?" Lane asked.

"At the corner store getting a cold drink. I suggested it after Christine had a meltdown."

Lane leaned forward, waiting for Arthur to continue.

"It started this morning, after Matt got up. He had no idea that Christine was here." Arthur put his wine down so he could tell more of the story with his hands. "He opened the bathroom door. Christine was sitting on the toilet. She screamed. Matt was embarrassed. He tried to apologize. It only made things worse."

"And?" Lane gulped his wine. *I can't believe it, I'm still thirsty after the sweat lodge,* he thought.

"Well, we got that settled. Then it was one thing after another until Christine started crying. One box of tissues later ..." Arthur plucked an imaginary tissue and pretended to dab his eyes "... we got that sorted out."

"What was there to sort out?"

"She's always lived around women. Apparently, the males in Paradise didn't want to have much to do with Christine. She kept saying that all of the pretty girls were blonde and ..." Arthur cupped his hands in front of his chest, moved them up, then held them there.

"I don't ..." Lane began.

Arthur shook his head with exasperation, "In case you hadn't noticed, Christine has a darker complexion and flatter chest than most." Arthur pointed a finger at his chest. "And I know what it's like growing up in small-town, lily-white Alberta with a better tan than anyone else around."

"You mean?" Lane held his left hand open.

"She was the only person with a tan in Paradise and an outsider because of it." Arthur reached for his wine and took a sip.

"I can't believe my sister would put up with that," Lane said.

"Neither could Christine. She thinks the colour of her skin had something to do with why Whitemore was going to excommunicate her." Arthur took a sip of wine. "And that's not all."

"There's more?" Lane rubbed his forehead with his forefinger and thumb.

"How come she asks permission to do everything including going to the bathroom?"

"What?"

Arthur used his left hand for emphasis. "It's not natural the way she wants to clean the house, do the dishes, and vacuum. It's too weird. When she's not crying, she's cleaning house."

Erinn held a sleeping Jessica in her arms. "There's something wrong with Glenn."

Harper hung his sports coat on the back of a kitchen chair. He rubbed his hand over the top of Jessica's head. Her hair tickled his palm. He leaned over, kissed Erinn and then Jessica. The baby sucked on an imagined breast.

"I'll go downstairs and see how Glenn is doing," he whispered.

The fifth stair creaked as he made his way downstairs. Glenn's door was closed.

Harper knocked.

No answer.

He knocked again. "Glenn?"

"I just want to be left alone. Please, leave me alone." Glenn's voice was just loud enough for Harper to hear.

"When can we talk?" Harper asked.

"Maybe tomorrow."

"There's more," Arthur said.

"More?"

"Matt wants to get a dog." Arthur hurried on. "I know how you feel, but it's time."

"No way. No dog," Lane said.

"You're outvoted on this one."

City Youth Struck by Freight Train

A seventeen-year-old male has been hit by a freight train. The train was westbound and approaching Edworthy Park when the young man was struck. He was killed instantly.

Traffic along the line was disrupted while police and railway officials investigated. The name of the victim will be released when next of kin have been notified.

chapter 4

Lane picked up the phone on the fourth ring. "Hello."

"We've got a body," Harper said. "How soon can I pick you up?"

"Thirty minutes." Lane looked at a frowning Arthur.

"Okay." Harper hung up.

"It's supposed to be your day off," Arthur said.

Lane rinsed his coffee cup and put it in the dishwasher. "I know, but I have to go."

"I need help with these kids." Arthur sat hunched over his coffee at the kitchen table.

Lane looked at Arthur. Having one teen around was taxing. Two were rapidly becoming overwhelming. He thought about the last ten months and what they'd lived through. Just when he was sure things were getting better, something else happened.

"I'll handle them, somehow." Arthur lifted his head and looked at Lane. "You'd better get ready."

"Where's the body?" Lane got in the Chev.

Harper handed him a cup of coffee. "Mochachino."

Lane took a sip and closed his eyes. "This is good." He reached for his seat belt.

"It's at the south end of the reservoir; Weaselhead. We're going to have to hike down. A jogger spotted it this morning at sunrise. The forensics team is already there." Harper pulled away from the curb and headed south.

"Have they identified the body?"

"Not yet. Rough night?" Harper sipped thoughtfully at his coffee.

"Two kids." Lane looked out the window.

"Lots of drama?"

"How did you know?" Lane looked left.

Harper pointed his cup at his chest. "Two kids."

Twenty minutes later, they threw their cups in the green bear-proof garbage containers at Weaselhead Park and drove past an open gate along a gravel road, then onto a paved bike trail. Harper parked alongside the police cruiser angled across the intersection of three pathways. A male officer manned the roadblock. He frowned.

Two joggers, one male and one female, dressed in matching red skintight shorts and tops, walked away from the barricade with their hands on their hips. "Man, this is gonna mess up my training schedule. Those hills are great for the calves," the man said.

The woman swigged from a water bottle, then replaced it in the loop nestled between the cheeks of her backside. "This'll screw my whole day up." She pulled out a cellphone and dialled.

Lane looked at Harper.

Harper shrugged, shook his head, and said, "Joggers," as if one word summed it up.

"Hope those two never have kids." The male officer nodded in the direction of the runners.

At the mention of kids, Lane thought about his home and wondered what it would look like when he got back.

"It ain't pretty down there," the officer said. "The

forensic unit is already on the scene. Want me to drive you down?"

"We'll walk," Lane said.

"Only takes about five minutes to walk anyway," the officer said.

"Thanks." Harper buttoned up his jacket.

They walked down the paved path as it dropped to the flats on the west end of Glenmore Reservoir. From the top of the path, they could see the river snaking through the mud flats before joining the deeper waters of the reservoir. To the south, about a kilometre away, the trail rose out of the valley and into a residential district.

Birdsong filtered through the trees. Leaves swayed in the gathering west wind that carried the scent of something unpleasant.

Harper looked at Lane as if to say, "Remember what we saw the last time we did this?"

They spotted the members of the Forensic Crime Scenes Unit at the far side of the pedestrian bridge. The body was under a yellow tarp a few metres from a power pole on the south bank of the river. A dark-haired woman wearing a ponytail, sweatpants, and tank top waited nearby with her black and tan dog. It sat with its head hung low.

"Dr. Fibre is waiting for us." Harper pointed at the doctor who stood in his white crime-scene bunny suit and rubber boots. "He doesn't look happy."

They walked along the bridge. The wind sang a haunting chorus as it sifted through the metal bars of the bridge railing.

Lane was watching the woman and her dog. She bent

at the waist. The dog lifted its head. It licked her face. The woman stood up straight, then yelled something unintelligible at the dog. The woman leaned forward and threw up. The dog cowered and dragged itself as far from the woman as the leash would allow.

Harper and Lane crossed the walking bridge and moved east along the Elbow River bank before reaching the scene.

"Colin Weaver." The doctor looked like an iconoclastic movie star, the kind whose face would be found on a poster portraying the actor as rebel. Dr. Weaver, or Dr. Fibre as everyone called him when he wasn't within shouting distance, had a conservative nature and the personality of a carpet. "This." Weaver was momentarily at a loss for words. "This is the person who discovered the body." Dr. Fibre pointed at the woman who was wiping her mouth with the back of her hand.

"I'll talk with her." Harper walked over to the woman.

Lane glanced at the dog. It looked at him with pitiful brown eyes. Lane studied the breed. *Looks like a cross between an Australian cattle dog and a German shepherd,* he thought.

"She's upset because she thinks her dog was eating the body. The evidence, however, suggests otherwise. It appears the dog was trying to drag the victim to safety. There are some marks on the wrist of the victim. But no puncture wounds or evidence of chewing. The dog was simply being a good Samaritan." Dr. Fibre walked over to the body.

Lane followed.

They both heard a helicopter approaching and looked up. It flew low over the water and hovered nearby. Lane waved it away. The yellow tarp was lifted by the helicopter's downdraft. The tarp flew off, was caught by the force of the west wind, and carried out into the mud flats. The naked body lay face down. Lane could see that the man had red hair.

Lane flipped open his phone and speed dialled. "We've got the traffic helicopter disturbing a crime scene. Get it out of here!"

Lane looked up at the pilot and waited. It took about thirty seconds before the pilot began to talk into his headset. The pilot looked at Lane, flipped him a middle finger, and flew away.

"That was unpleasant." Dr. Fibre watched the helicopter leave.

"We won't have much time, now." Lane moved next to Fibre and looked at the body. The skin was discoloured next to the spine, at an angle between the shoulder blades. There were early signs of decomposition and the corpse didn't match the missing person's description.

"I noticed that as well," Fibre said as if reading Lane's mind. "The hair colour does not match the missing man's. Nor does the height and weight estimate. No one mentioned a tattoo on Mr. Dudley. As you can see, the deceased has a tattoo circling his right bicep. The cause of death appears, initially at least, to be blunt trauma to the parietal bone."

Lane looked at the way the skull was concave at the back on one side. "All it tells us is that the assailant was probably right-handed."

"It's too early for me to tell if the death will be classified as murder. It is definitely suspicious, however," Fibre said.

"There was no clothing found nearby?" Lane looked along the river's edge. *The lack of clothing and the blunt trauma to the back of the head mean this was almost certainly murder,* Lane thought. *A blow like that would make the victim incapable of undressing himself.*

"None." Dr. Fibre waved at the two men combing the edge of the river. "I suspect the body was very recently immersed. The lack of advanced decomposition and the fact that scavengers have not begun to feed on the remains would tend to suggest that. It's time to move the body and complete an autopsy."

"Will you call me with the findings?" Lane asked.

Fibre nodded and walked away.

I guess the conversation is over, Lane thought. *It's time for us to find out the identity of a second missing person.*

Fibre's assistants moved in to bag the body.

Lane walked back toward Harper. He was watching the woman leave with her dog.

"Man, she's really upset. She found her dog and the body at the same time. She still thinks Cal, the dog, was snacking on the remains." Harper watched the body being wrapped. "Is that Dudley?"

Lane shook his head. "Doesn't appear to be. And Fibre thinks the dog was just trying to drag the body out of the water."

They walked back to the path and across the bridge. Ahead of them, the woman pulled viciously on the dog's leash. It yelped with pain.

"The dog is just a pup. The witness said it was five months old. Some kind of Australian cattle dog." Harper was becoming uncomfortable with Lane's silence.

"Sorry," Lane said, "it's just that we had a missing person and no body. Now we have a body and no missing person. And we're just downstream from where Eva and Blake live. I was sure we were going to find Ryan Dudley's body."

They walked up the hill to the parking lot. As they reached the police barricade, the officer said, "You missed all the excitement. Some lady took her dog's collar and leash off, then drove away. The poor dog went running after her car down 37th Street." He pointed north as SUVs turned into the parking lot of Weaselhead Park. Both had the logos of rival television news stations painted along their flanks.

"Thanks for hanging around to help me deal with the media, guys," the officer said as he saw the detectives move quickly toward their car.

Harper and Lane climbed into the Chevy. Harper waved at the reporters as they drove alongside.

"I'm telling you, that old Indian woman is responsible for the disappearances. Eva is her name. Yes, it's Eva Star something or other," Sophia Lombardi said.

Lane had taken her call just after four in the afternoon. Sophia was in a panic because she couldn't locate her brother. "Her last name wouldn't be Starchild?"

"That's it! That's her!" Sophia's voice rose in volume and pitch.

"When did you last talk to your brother?" Lane jotted notes as they talked.

"Last week. We met for lunch. We were supposed to meet today at noon. I phoned his work. He never arrived today. I phoned him and left messages. First Duds disappeared and now Skip. Not to mention Tyler. I mean, they've been friends for a long time. Lived together just on the edge of the city with Blake. He told me it was Eva Starchild who was behind all of this. You'd better arrest her before Blake goes missing too. Skip told me they were sure she was the one." Sophia took a breath.

"What does your brother look like?" Lane asked.

"Red hair, medium height and build. Has a tattoo up high on his right arm. Looks like barbed wire. He works out," Sophia said.

"Do you have a photograph?" Lane tried to keep his voice even as he thought, *The odds are pretty good that your brother is dead.*

"Yes."

"Would you mind bringing it downtown?" *And I'll probably have to ask you to identify your brother's body.*

"I'll be there in half an hour. It's Detective Lane, right?"

"That's correct."

Sophia hung up.

Lane looked at Harper, who sat at the next desk. "It looks like we have a connection between the body found this morning and the two missing persons."

chapter 5

Aidan wore a blue-black tux with tails. Her shirt was red silk and the tie a silvery blue. Her blonde hair was wet and slicked back. Her capris were skintight and reached halfway down her calves. The pantyhose underneath were the same shade as the tie. Her shoes (more like hiking boots) were red with black toes and soles. She stood atop a metal catwalk running above a series of wooden cases holding marionettes in various costumes and poses. One of the cases remained closed. On the floor was a black cloth with highway dashes painted on it in yellow.

The yard light above her head was all that lit the stage. It cast long shadows as Aidan walked Alex, the marionette, to centre stage. He was dressed in the colours of the rainbow, finished off with a pair of jaca-randa-purple shoes.

Then, Aidan's marionette (dressed exactly like Aidan) walked onstage from the opposite direction. The pair of marionettes stood face to face.

Alex was animated. Aidan, the marionette, assumed the pose of someone listening.

"How come you're all dressed up and I'm wearing this?" Alex pointed at his shirt.

"You know me, I'm trying to resurrect the drag-king phenomena. That way the guys in the audience will be able to get some fashion tips while watching the show. And, I thought you might enjoy the coming out symbols and colours...."

"Okay. Okay. I get it!"

"What's your problem?" Aidan asked.

Alex tuned his back on her and crossed his arms. "You didn't go to my sweat."

"I'm sorry." Aidan the marionette and Aidan the person hung their heads.

"Was it your moon time?" Alex turned his head.

"Yes."

Alex turned to face her. "Well, then you couldn't have been there anyway. You're too powerful at that time of the month."

Aidan's faces lifted to see Alex. "Still, I wanted to be there. I know I said it was the cops, but it wasn't. That's when I can feel closest to you. You come to the sweat to be next to me."

"Careful, people will begin to think I'm a ghost." Alex held his hands up in the air.

"Just the ones who don't understand."

"That we were like brother and sister?" Alex let his arms drop slowly to his sides.

"You understand."

"And you're worried about my grandmother, aren't you?" Alex placed a hand on Aidan's marionette shoulder.

"She did get those threats on her computer," Aidan said.

"She'll be okay. She's not the one responsible," Alex said.

"You know who it is?" Aidan's eyes opened wide.

"Of course. I saw what you couldn't see." Alex took his hand away and smiled.

"And you're not gonna tell me, right?" Aidan shook her head.

"Maybe during the show. See how I feel. See what the audience is like. So, are we going to get on with the dress rehearsal or what?" Alex put his hands on his hips.

"Okay. You're the boss!" Aidan's voice rose with expectation and exasperation.

"Well, if I'm the boss I demand a new wardrobe!" Alex lifted one shoe for emphasis. "And I wanna do some dancing in one of the scenes."

"We'll see." Aidan looked in the direction of the audience.

"What does that mean?" Alex looked out into the darkness as if trying to see what she was seeing.

"It means we'll see. You keep secrets from me, so that means I get to keep a few from you."

ch*a*pter 6

Lane found himself in the middle of a domestic war. Arthur's eyes were wide with a combination of shock and disbelief.

Matt's face was red with rage and his voice distorted by it. "What the hell did you do to my room?" He stood in the middle of the kitchen.

"I cleaned it." Christine's response was matter-of-fact as she turned to face him.

"You had no right!" Matt was close to tears. "It's my room, not yours. Who the hell do you think you are?"

"It was a mess." Christine smiled.

"You bitch!" Matt turned his back and pounded downstairs.

Christine followed.

Lane tried to hold her back, grabbed at her arm, but she shrugged him off.

"Don't you call me that! Don't you ever call me that!" Christine was two steps behind Matt.

Matt's door slammed.

"Open this door!" There was a violent tearing of wood. The hollow core door to Matt's room caved in when Christine put her foot through it.

"We're going to the animal shelter tomorrow. The kids want to pick out a dog." Arthur delivered the message with the finality of the twelfth commandment.

Lane had just finished talking to Christine about the repair for the door and had yet to talk with Matt. His mind was filled with today's happenings at work and a single-minded desire for a shower. "You mean Matt wants to pick out a dog."

"No. That's the funny thing. This is the first thing they've agreed on since Christine came here, despite what happened tonight. Since we're on the topic of Christine, have you looked at her room? It's spotless. She insists on cleaning her room, and the rest of the house, each and every morning." Arthur took a breath. "And we're going to the rodeo. All of us."

"First off, what's so bad about Christine cleaning house?" Lane sat down on an oak kitchen chair.

"Besides the fact that she does a better job than me?"

Lane began to respond and stopped when he realized there was no way to answer the question without getting into more trouble.

"She asks permission to do everything. To wash her hands, wash the floors, take a bath, brush her teeth."

"I don't …"

"That's right you don't understand. The kid's like a trained circus animal. She seldom leaves the house, is afraid to make a decision on her own, and yet she's busting out, just itching to fight. I mean look at her clothes! What the heck is going on with that?"

"What do you want me to do?" Lane surrendered.

"Come with us tomorrow to look at dogs. And make time for the rodeo. It's not very far away."

"Can I have a shower now?" Lane asked.

Arthur's entire manner softened. "How bad was it?"

"A body in the Elbow River, having the body identified, a sister who collapsed after she saw the body. Pretty bad." Lane related the information in a flat, matter-of-fact tone.

"Sorry." Arthur put his hand on Lane's shoulder then a palm to his cheek. "Then you come home and walk into a battle between the kids. Still, we have to go for the dog tomorrow. I promised."

"Okay." Lane thought, *How come your promises become mine?* He got up and headed for the shower. "By the way, don't we owe Lisa and Loraine a dinner?"

"How come when *you* have to talk with Lisa about a case, *I* always end up cooking dinner?"

Lane kept moving down the hall. "Just lucky, I guess."

"He's downstairs sleeping it off." Erinn rubbed her hand across her face. When she took her hand away, there were dark semicircles reclining under each eye.

Harper sat down on the opposite side of the table. "What happened?"

"He came home drunk, sat down in your chair, and started talking." Erinn's red hair sprouted out at odd angles. She wasn't smiling.

"About what?" Harper almost said something about her hair before thinking better of it.

"His friend died." Erinn looked at Harper like he was the first or second stupidest person on the planet.

"What?" Harper felt he was just beginning to understand.

"Didn't you read the paper?" Erinn asked.

"What do you mean?" Harper held his hands out, palms up.

"The kid who was hit by the train was Glenn's friend." Erinn wiped the back of her hand across her eyes.

"Shit." Harper stood and moved closer to hold her.

Erinn leaned against him. "We have to go to the rodeo. Arthur invited us. Glenn wants to go. Maybe it'll put a smile back on his face. He's so down."

Later, Harper awoke to Jessica's crying. He opened his eyes to see the illuminated time on the alarm clock. It read three-thirty AM.

Erinn snored.

He rolled out of bed, pulled on a T-shirt and sweats. When he turned on the light in Jessica's room, she had a fist jammed in her mouth. He went to pick her up and found that her pajamas were wet from the armpits down. He carried her to the changing table and pulled out a diaper and clean pajamas. As he worked Jessica's arms and feet out of the pajamas, he heard footsteps in the hall. Without looking, Harper said, "It's okay Erinn, go back to sleep. She's just wet."

"Can't sleep." Glenn's voice sounded like it had been tuned with beer and secondhand cigarette smoke. He moved into Jessica's room.

"You smell like a brewery." Harper dropped the wet pajamas in the hamper. He held his hand on Jessica's tummy while studying Glenn's slow, deliberate motions.

"I know. I look like shit." Glenn leaned against the door jam.

Harper took off Jessica's diaper. Glenn lifted the lid of the garbage can. Harper dropped the diaper inside. Glenn closed the lid. He covered his mouth and gagged.

In a minute, Harper had the baby in fresh pajamas and tucked next to his ribs. The three of them made for the kitchen.

"Better have some breakfast. Get something in your stomach." Harper washed one hand after the other in the kitchen sink, juggled Jessica from one arm to the next, filled the coffee maker with water, and reached for a filter.

Glenn sat down and put his head on the table. "They say he had his music on."

"What?" Harper measured out the coffee. "What are you talking about?"

Glenn lifted his head.

Harper closed the lid on the coffee machine, turned it on, and sat down across from Glenn.

Glenn smiled at Jessica. "Her eyes are closing."

Harper waited.

Glenn's smile died. "Steven had his music turned way up so he couldn't hear the train. Don't know how he ignored the vibration, the horn, or the headlight."

"He was your friend?"

Jessica pulled at the hairs on Harper's arm.

Glenn nodded. There were tears in his eyes.

The coffee maker spluttered.

"Any idea why?" Harper kept his voice low.

"He knew that I'm gay. We used to talk about it. He told me how his parents were pretty religious and opinionated about lifestyle choices, if you know what I mean." Glenn's eyes were red-rimmed as he looked at his uncle.

"You mean they were homophobes?" Harper gently caressed Jessica's head with his lips. Her eyes closed.

"Yep. Anyway, he was feeling down about a week ago. I saw him at school after an exam. We chatted for a few minutes, then he left. That was the last time I saw him. I got a call yesterday. The funeral date hasn't been set yet."

"You're not responsible." Harper stood up.

"Remember when I dressed up in drag for Halloween, and the principal told me to change or go home?"

For a moment Harper thought Glenn was going to laugh and say, "Change into what? I mean I am who I am, right?"

Instead, Glenn said, "Steven was the one who told me to come to school the next day dressed in that three-piece pinstriped business suit. He told me it would make a statement louder than any argument. He taught me how to fight back. Even brought me an old black leather briefcase to carry with the suit."

"It's not your fault." Harper moved closer to Glenn.

Glenn shrugged. His eyes filled with tears. His hands covered his face and he began to sob. Glenn woke Jessica, who began to cry in sympathy. Harper stood there in the middle of the kitchen, not knowing what to do next.

Disappearances Cause Stampede Concern

Unsolved disappearances and the discovery of the body of an as yet unidentified white male have created ripples within the city and surrounding communities. The unsolved disappearances of Ryan Dudley and Tyler McNally have been overshadowed by the discovery of a third body. Dudley competed as a bull rider before his disappearance. McNally often accompanied Dudley on the rodeo circuit. Both men lived together.

A roommate of the two men, Blake Rogers, said, "Duds was a real competitor. He and Tyler were real tight. Whoever is behind what happened to them better be careful. Cowboys are slow to get mad, but once that happens, watch out."

Questions were raised by representatives of the Calgary Stampede Board. They expressed concern that patrons may stay away from this year's Stampede due to security concerns. As a result, fifty more security guards have been hired. Also, there will be an increased police presence on the grounds.

ch*a*pter 7

Lane thought, *You look like hell.* "How's the coffee?"

Harper and Lane sat across from one another in a coffee shop at the edge of town. Kuldeep was behind the counter. She smiled as she served the coffee. She thanked them in a now familiar voice that was one part music and one part English.

Harper looked over his double espresso as he took a sip and burned his tongue. He shook his head. They sat next to the window. The morning sun warmed the east side of their faces.

"Rough night?" Lane asked.

Harper looked back at Lane as if to say, "You don't know the half of it."

"Want to talk?" Lane asked.

"Did you read about the kid hit by the train down by Edworthy Park?"

Lane felt a sense of dread working its way up from his belly. "Yes."

"It was a friend of Glenn's. Name was Steven. Apparently the kid was talking about coming out. Glenn thinks the talk didn't go well with Steven's parents so he killed himself. Glenn's blaming himself."

"Believe me, Glenn's not responsible." Lane looked through Harper and into the past where memories of other tragedies created whitewater waves around boulders in the treacherous river of his early years.

"I guess Steven put his headphones on, turned up the music, and walked down the railway tracks." Harper put his cup down. "It happened a couple of nights ago."

Lane couldn't think of anything to say, opened his mouth to say something anyway, then shut it.

"There's nothing you can say." Harper looked out the window. "Jessica and Glenn cried off and on for a couple of hours this morning. One would stop and the other would get started again. Erinn slept through the whole thing."

"Matt wants a dog," Lane said.

"What?" Harper looked at Lane like he hadn't heard correctly.

"We have to go to the animal shelter tonight to look for a dog."

"Oh?" It was Harper's turn to be lost for words. He remembered what happened during last October's snowstorm and what he'd found when he went looking for Lane's dog, Riley.

"I don't know," Lane said.

"Man, you've been weird ever since the sweat lodge."

Thankfully, Lane's phone rang. "Hello."

Lane looked at Harper. "We're on our way."

Fifteen silent minutes later, they were headed west toward the mountains, the very edge of town where the city and the country rubbed up against one another. Lane noticed a gas station on the north side of the highway as they passed it. It was a rare example of nineteen fifties' architecture. The metal shone and the stucco had a fresh coat of white paint. *I wonder how long before it gets torn down?* he thought.

Lane looked down the two lane highway. He broke the silence, picking up where their conversation had ended at the coffee shop. "How weird have I been acting?"

"Out there. Distracted. You know, distant. Thinking about something else all the time. What happened to you?"

Lane thought for a minute. "I still haven't figured that out. When I do, I'll let you know."

Harper decided not to push it. "Is Fibre gonna be there?"

"He's on his way."

They turned south onto the gravel road leading to Blake Rogers' acreage.

Lane could feel the sweat gathering along his hairline when they got out of the air-conditioned car and faced Blake's ranch-style house with its red brick front. He stood next to the car and waited for Rosco the German shepherd. In the quiet, he listened to the ticking of the car's cooling engine. He heard Harper moving his feet on the gravel. Lane looked across at his partner. Harper was checking and rechecking every shrub, every corner, every bit of cover where someone might hide near the ranch house.

Blake opened the door. Lane watched him step out into the sun. Again, Blake was dressed in black. He put on his black stetson.

"Morning detectives. It's Harper and?…" Blake motioned with his right hand.

"Detective Lane," Harper said.

"We need to go around back." Blake led the way to the south side of the house.

Lane looked at the Quonset and corral. There were no horses or cattle. Grass grew knee-high inside the fence. He could see no evidence of trampled or grazed grass.

They followed Blake around to the back of the house.

"Didn't find these 'til this morning. I got up and went to check the yard." Blake pointed at the white vinyl siding.

"Where's Rosco?" Lane asked.

Blake looked away. "Don't know."

Lane and Harper looked back at the house. The bullet holes were relatively evenly spaced, working their way from the lower north side of the wall up to where one round had shattered a roof tile at the south peak of one gable. Lane counted five bullet holes.

"Didn't hit any windows." Harper looked at Blake before looking back at Lane with his best "I don't buy it" look.

"That's why I didn't notice it last night," Blake said.

Lane walked north to the stacked round bails about twenty metres from the north end of the house.

"There's a guy who cuts the hay for us. He takes a percentage for his cattle. Duds liked to feed it to his horse." Blake followed along behind Lane.

Harper followed Blake.

Lane turned and studied the ground.

Blake said, "What you lookin' for?"

"Whatever is here." Lane said the words without looking back at Blake.

"Does Rosco do this often?" Lane looked at the ground while listening intently to Blake's tone of voice.

He's not so cocky all of a sudden, Lane thought. *What's caused the change in behaviour?*

"What? What are you talkin' about?" Blake asked.

"Does Rosco often disappear for a day or two?" Harper asked.

"You never can tell about a dog." Blake delivered the reply like a joke.

"Dogs get hungry." Lane stopped, looked back at the house to get his bearings. He looked at the stack of bails. One sat on its end while the others lay on their sides stacked end to end, making one long cylinder. He spotted a glint of something on the upright bail. He walked to the stack. The hay crop whispered against his pant legs as he moved. The ground was uneven and soft underfoot.

"What do you see?" Blake's voice was pitched higher.

Harper and Blake followed until they stood next to Lane by the bail. Lane reached over and pointed at a dime-sized piece of glass at the top of the bail. He showed it to Harper.

Harper looked at Blake. "Do you do any target shooting?"

"Never." Blake shook his head emphatically.

"The forensic team will be here soon. We'll wait for them." Lane looked down and found a shard of glass about a metre from the bail.

"You know who did this, don't you?" Blake asked.

"Nope," Harper said.

"It's obvious. Eva Starchild's been behind this from the beginning." Blake folded his arms, then leaned defiantly against a bail.

Harper drove into Eva's back yard. There was one car parked near the garage.

Lane looked at the fire pit where the rocks for the sweat lodge were heated. The air above the pit wasn't wavering from the heat.

"Think she heard us comin'?" Harper smiled before calling in their location.

To Lane's ears, the Chev's doors sounded unnaturally loud when they closed.

Their feet crunched on the sand and gravel driveway.

The first rap of Harper's knuckles made the back door shudder. He looked over his shoulder at Lane, then tapped with a polite tattoo.

Eva opened the door, smiled then nodded at Lane as if to say, "I've been expecting you."

"Can we talk with you?" Lane asked.

"Come." Eva was wearing a blue nightgown and a white hand-knit sweater. She turned, then walked up the stairs and into the kitchen.

Lane stepped inside and looked at the landing. Pairs of shoes lay scattered there. He looked at Eva's feet. She wore slippers.

Lane bent to untie his shoes. He turned to Harper who looked at Lane, uncertain what to do next. They looked up the stairs. Eva was watching.

Harper took his shoes off.

Eva smiled. "Just cleaned the floor yesterday."

Lane looked at the green linoleum. It shone despite the patches where traffic had worn it down to the black. He stepped inside the kitchen and noticed the pot of coffee on the stove. There was the scent of something else too. *Baking in the oven*, Lane thought.

"Coffee?" Eva asked.

"Sure," Lane said.

"Cream? Sugar?" Eva opened the cupboard.

"Please," Harper said.

"Sit." Eva cocked her head to the right.

Lane and Harper sat down at the kitchen table in one of the eight assorted wooden chairs surrounding it. The pictures of hummingbirds, Aidan and Alex, Norm on a brand new all-terrain vehicle and a dancing Alex hung on the wall behind Harper.

Harper watched Lane, who looked back with a blank expression. *Just be patient*, Lane thought and hoped Harper got the message.

Eva brought sugar and a jug of milk to the table along with three coffee cups of assorted colours and designs. She poured coffee before returning to the stove. Fresh-baked muffins and butter appeared. "Been expecting you."

"What kind of muffins? They smell great," Harper said.

"Saskatoon." Eva sat across from them.

Lane's mouth watered.

Eva lifted her black coffee and sipped. She closed her eyes.

Lane buttered a muffin. "You were expecting us?"

"Yep." Eva eyed him impassively as she took another sip.

Harper devoured his saskatoon muffin and reached for a second.

Lane waited.

Eva waited.

Harper ate a third muffin. "Okay if I get more coffee?"

Eva nodded.

"How long are we going to sit like this?" Lane asked.

"My house." Eva intended the two words to carry a wide range of meanings, the most obvious of which was, "Until I'm good and ready."

Harper ate a fourth muffin. "These are amazing." A piece of muffin popped out of his mouth onto the table. He grabbed it and put it in his mouth, then looked to see if Eva had noticed. His lips were stained purple.

Eva smiled. She looked in Harper's direction. "He's okay. Talks too much, but he's okay."

Lane nodded in agreement.

"You're here because someone shot at that Blake Rogers' house," Eva said.

"How did you know?" Harper asked.

"Somebody always sees what's going on out here even when there's nobody around." Eva got up to pour herself some more coffee. "More?"

"Please," Lane said.

"Me too." Harper spit bits of muffin and raised his cup. "You hear the shots?"

"Nope." Eva warmed their cups, then refilled her own.

"How did you know, then?" Lane asked.

"Same as most people. Phone call."

Lane laughed. "From who?"

"A friend."

Lane said, "Rogers thinks you did it."

"Course he does." Eva smirked.

Lane held his hands with the palms up to indicate he was trying to understand.

"Don't own a gun. Won't have one in the house or on my land. Go and take a look if you like." She said this as if they'd be wasting their time.

"If there's no gun, then you've got nothing to worry about," Harper said.

"Home alone last night." Eva waited as they chewed that piece of news over.

"Nobody came around?" Harper wiped his mouth with his hand.

"Nope. Not even Norm. He was home watching TV."

"Bad blood between you and Blake Rogers?" Lane asked.

"Might say that." Eva put her coffee cup down and wrapped her fingers around it, keeping them warm.

"Do you want to tell us why?" Lane watched Eva's eyes. They were beginning to fill with tears.

Eva took a long breath. "Do you want to tell us about the vision you had at the sweat lodge?"

Lane sat back. He thought, *That question caught me completely by surprise.* He looked closer at Eva. "How did you know?"

"You had that look when you left the sweat. Real thoughtful, like you'd seen something you'd never seen before. Seen that look a time or two. Even seen it in the mirror a time or two. It's the way people look after a vision." Eva waited for Lane's reaction.

"You're right. Something happened. I can't explain it." The room got warmer. Lane felt sweat gathering along his hairline. And more dripping down his ribs.

"Try." Eva leaned closer.

"It felt like my grandfather was there next to me. But he's been dead for more than twenty-five years," Lane said. "He taught me that looking out for kids was the most important thing an adult can do. He always watched out for me."

"You know Alex, my grandson, was killed by a pickup truck. Some boys drove onto the side of the road and opened their door. Ran him down like a dog. Killed him. He couldn't hear them comin'. Alex was deaf." Tears ran down Eva's cheeks. She wiped them away. "I wasn't watching close enough."

"I read the reports," Harper said.

"Blake Rogers was behind it all," Eva said.

"How do you know?" Lane asked.

"Same way you know your grandfather was with you at the sweat. Sometimes my grandson, my Alex, comes to the sweat just to comfort me. I invite him, just like you invited your grandfather." Eva wiped at her nose with a Kleenex pulled from her sleeve. "I can feel it the way I can feel a hummingbird when it passes close by. Like the wind of its wings washing against my face."

"Did anyone else know Blake killed your grandson?" Harper asked.

"Lots of people. No one could prove it, but they knew all the same." After that, Eva said very little.

Lane and Harper got up to leave after fifteen minutes of uncomfortable silence.

Eva came outside. Lane motioned for Eva to go first as they stepped through the gate. Harper pointed at the evergreens planted in a line. "I wanted to ask you about those trees."

Eva stepped outside the gate. "Ask."

The first bullet slapped into the Chev's gas tank.

Eva dodged to her right.

Harper tackled Lane.

Lane felt the blow just below his ribs. The air was forced from his lungs. His face was shoved into the gravel.

For several moments, Lane struggled to get his breath back. He spit gravel and dirt. Lane sat up and leaned his back against the front tire where they were protected by the car's engine.

Harper crouched next to him with his Glock drawn. He looked for Eva but couldn't spot her. The next bullet took out the rear tire on the far side of the car. The air filled with gasoline fumes.

"Where is he?" Harper asked.

"Thought I heard the shot. It sounded a long way off. And it sounds like a small calibre. Maybe a twenty-two." Lane pulled his Glock out of its holster with one hand and his cellphone out with the other.

A minute later the gas tank was punctured again. Lane heard the bullet hum as it ricocheted off a rock and smacked into something nearby. The spark of the ricochet ignited the fumes from the leaking tank. Flames spilled around the back of the car and cooked the rear of the Chev's underbelly.

Harper grabbed Lane by the arm. They crouched and ran back though the gate and around the side of the house, where Eva found them.

"Have another coffee." She handed each of them a mug. "He's gone."

"You sure?" Harper asked.

"Yep." Eva waited with them and watched the flames boil around the rear of the car. "You're hurt." She looked at Lane and the blood on the ground.

He felt his ribs. By the time he got around to feeling his backside, his hand came away bloody. "Great."

Eva went back in the house and came back with a tea towel. Lane used it to apply pressure to the wound.

Lane leaned the back of his head against the side of the house. Motion at the south side of Eva's yard attracted his attention. A blur of wings hovered near purple honeysuckle. Lane thought, *What is that?* "Over there; it's a hummingbird."

Harper turned when Lane pointed.

The bird stuck its beak deep into the flower.

Lane watched, fascinated, realizing he'd never actually seen a hummingbird before.

The black column of smoke guided the emergency vehicles to the scene. Within thirty minutes the yard was was filled with an ambulance, two fire engines, assorted police vehicles, and Dr. Fibre's forensic unit.

"You should learn to let it go." Alex was using his most annoying holier-than-thou voice. "I can't even remember any pain. One minute I'm looking at you, I feel a vibration; there wasn't even time to turn before the door hit me. That was it. Pretty painless, really."

Aidan crouched atop the catwalk. She wore red for this scene. A blood-red satin blouse, red jeans, socks, and shoes. Even a red ball cap.

Aidan's marionette was dressed the same way. She said, "But I still feel guilty. If I hadn't distracted you …"

"See, that's what I mean! You blame yourself. This guilt eats away at you from the inside. The guys in the truck meant for it to happen, not you!" Alex raised his arms in exasperation. "The only thing you should feel guilty about is this damned outfit you put me in!" He used his hands to point at the rainbow of colours. "I never wore anything like this in my life!"

"It's symbolic!" Aidan the marionette pointed at the sky for effect.

"And she chooses the wardrobes! She wears those amazing outfits and I'm stuck with this!" Alex put his hands on his hips and looked up at Aidan the puppeteer.

She looked down and smiled. "I want the audience to really see me. You know, so they can't miss me. Then when the transformation comes, if it comes, when the audience forgets I'm here, that's what I'll be waiting for."

"Transformation?" Alex looked out where the audience would be.

"When you become real. When the audience sees each marionette as a real person. Someone who lives and breathes. That's what needs to happen."

Alex looked back at Aidan the marionette. "So what difference will that make? How will that change what happened, what's still happening? Everyone knew whose truck it was, even though you didn't see the rear plate. The problem was the police couldn't prove it, that's all! By the time the RCMP got around to checking the pickup, both doors were replaced with new ones." Alex smiled and looked at the audience. "They had a body and a witness but no conclusive evidence.

Four guys living together in one house. All four knew what they did to me. Not one of them talked. All they were worried about was saving their skins. And I was called the 'victim of the week'!"

"I'm almost there." Lane had his cellphone wedged between his shoulder and his left ear. One hand lifted him up to keep his right cheek off the car seat. The other leaned against the back of the seat. He winced as he used his left hand to reach around and shut the phone off.

"Hurtin'?" Harper asked.

Lane inhaled. "Yes."

"You didn't tell him." Harper turned off Deerfoot Trail where the uneven surface of the roadway created a choppy, tortuous ride.

"Arthur's had enough trouble this year. He doesn't need another phone call like that. He still jumps every time the phone rings. For a long time after his sister and after the fire, he couldn't sleep. Kept wandering around the house at night. He needs to see me face to face." Lane shifted his backside. The pain came in a series of crescendos swelling to a climax with the pumping of his heart.

"Your face isn't looking all that great either. While one doctor was picking the bullet out of your butt, another one was picking gravel from your cheek. Want to stop for some painkillers?"

"I took two pills a half hour ago. They haven't started to work yet."

Harper glanced up. He caught a glimpse of a twin-engined passenger jet lining up its approach for landing.

White vapour trails streamed from its flaps and wing-tips. "You think *you've* got some explaining to do? Wait 'til *I* get home."

Lane smiled. "Better than the alternative, I guess." He thought, *Finally, the pain is easing.*

Harper laughed. "There's always that." He dropped Lane off in front of the glass and concrete structure of the Animal Shelter. Arthur's Jeep was parked out front in the parking lot.

"Good luck. And we need to talk about the case in a day or two. There's something we need to figure out," Harper said.

"What?" Lane asked, then watched Harper drive away. He limped up to the front door of the shelter and stepped inside. *What did Harper mean by that?*

He caught the scent of disinfectant first. *Almost smells like the Emergency ward.* Lane looked right at an artificial waterfall then left down a hallway with individual rooms for dogs. Concentrating on walking a straight line, he followed the hallway to a room with glass walls where he spotted Arthur, Matt, and Christine.

Arthur bent over a dog sitting between Matt and Christine. The dog was about a third of the size of a German shepherd, with similar markings.

Lane blinked. His stomach heaved with nausea, then settled when he took a deep breath. He thought, *The pills are taking the edge off of the pain.*

Matt rubbed the dog under its chin. It closed its eyes.

Christine rubbed the dog behind the ears.

Matt glared at her.

Lane thought, *The ears are a little big and the nose a little long. It's almost fox-like. There's something familiar about this dog.*

"Owner abandoned it." A woman dressed in a blue top and pants stood next to Lane. She said, "All the dogs have a microchip now. We called the owner up when we found her dog. It was found running down Glenmore Trail. The dog caused a traffic jam when it lay down in the middle of the road. The owner said she wanted nothing more to do with it. Something about the dog being untrainable."

Lane stared at the woman in the blue outfit. Her name tag introduced her as WANDA. There was a layer of makeup between her and Lane. He found himself fascinated by her blue eye shadow. It was as if he was seeing the colour for the first time.

"She sure likes your family." Wanda pointed.

Lane looked at the dog. It turned its head to study him. Arthur, Christine and Matt turned to see what caught the dog's eye. Their mouths fell open in unison.

Lane looked down at his clothing. He was wearing a light blue sweatshirt and evergreen sweatpants. Someone, he couldn't remember who, had loaned him the outfit. *After all,* he thought, *his pants were ruined and the jacket sent off to the cleaners. Perfectly understandable under the circumstances.* Lane tried to remember if an emergency nurse or doctor had helped him remove his tie and shirt. *They were a Christmas gift from Arthur. What happened to them?* he thought.

"What happened to you?"

Lane looked over at Arthur, who opened the door to the glass room. He was frowning.

"Nothin'." Lane found that his mind was about two or three steps behind what he was seeing, what he was hearing. He looked over his shoulder, wondering if he could ask Wanda exactly what colour her eye shadow was.

"You look like …" Arthur said, then looked at Matt.

"Hell." Matt finished Arthur's sentence.

"It didn't go in very far. Just tissue damage. Not close to any vital organs. Well, maybe one." *Or is it three?* he thought. Lane looked to Christine and Matt for help.

"Your face. Uncle Lane, what happened to your face?" Matt asked.

"Harper knocked me down. There was gravel on the driveway." Lane made a descending motion with his right hand in an attempt to mimic his face-first dive behind the car.

"Why would your partner do that?" Christine asked.

"Exactly what I was thinking." Arthur looked closely at Lane's face.

Lane's mind ran ahead then lagged behind, trying to catch up to three conversations. "The doctor said I'd probably notice some bruising in a day or two. I can go to Dr. Keeler to have the stitches removed."

"I don't see any stitches," Matt said.

"Neither do I," Christine said.

Lane remembered thinking that what he did next seemed perfectly logical at the time. He turned around and pointed at the backside of his borrowed sweatpants before pulling down one side to expose the damaged cheek. *That way everyone can have a look at the wound, or, rather, the dressing,* he thought. *Put all of the confusion to an end, as it were.* Lane grinned at his private joke.

Christine screamed, "You're bleeding!"

Matt said, "Uncle Lane, do you always go commando?"

The dog lay at the very back of the Jeep. "Her paws are still healing," Wanda had said. "The poor thing needs rest and a good home."

Christine and Matt sat as far away from each other as the back seat of the Jeep would allow.

Arthur drove while Lane watched the colours go by. *When did the world get so beautiful?* he thought.

"How come you didn't call?" Arthur asked as they turned from McKnight Boulevard onto John Laurie.

"I didn't want to upset everyone. Once you saw I was on my feet, you wouldn't worry so much. If I called, you'd worry too much." Lane stared at a shade of green he'd never seen before.

"So instead, with your face all scratched and bruised, you decide to arrive at the Animal Shelter and moon us!" Arthur changed into the right lane without signalling. A horn sounded from behind. Matt turned and flipped the driver a middle finger.

Lane thought, *I never realized that there were so many shades of green.* He felt the seat belt tighten across his chest and abdomen.

"What's he doing?" Arthur skidded off the road and stopped with the front of the Jeep pointed uphill.

Lane looked left. A white Ford pickup had cut them off and forced them onto the grass. The passenger got out. He was holding what looked like a half metre of wooden shovel handle.

Lane opened his door.

Arthur said, "Stay inside. Lock the doors!"

Lane looked at the man with the shovel handle. He was a head shorter than Lane and wore a pair of khaki coveralls.

Lane undid his seatbelt. "I'm a police officer."

The driver of the Ford rounded the front of the pickup. He was shorter than the man in the coveralls but looked like he worked out. "Bullshit! Let's see your badge!"

Lane reached for his pocket and thought, *What did I do with my ID?*

"He is a police officer!" Arthur got out of the Jeep. His voice was pitched high with fear.

The Ford driver smiled. "Where did you learn to drive? Flamer school? This should be fun, Randy. We've got a couple of sweethearts here. Haven't you heard? God doesn't like people like you or her for that matter." The driver pointed at Christine, who was climbing out of the Jeep.

Lane saw Randy step toward him. He heard Matt say, "Watch out, Uncle!"

Randy raised the shovel handle.

Lane moved inside the arc of the weapon. He reached out to grab Randy's right wrist with his left hand. With his right hand, Lane grabbed Randy by the throat. Lane's right foot hooked behind Randy's leg. The look on Randy's face changed from arrogance to shock as he landed flat on his back with Lane's knee on his chest. The wooden handle rolled down the slope.

The driver of the Ford ran toward Lane. Arthur grabbed the driver from behind. The driver swung at Arthur, but Matt caught a hold of the man's arm before it could connect with Arthur's head.

The driver swung around and threw Matt up the embankment.

Arthur let go and faced the driver.

The driver smiled. "Wrong move, girly-boy."

There was a hollow thud when the shovel handle caught the driver at an angle between his shoulder blades. The blow drove him to his knees.

A car horn sounded.

"I hate people like you!" Christine raised the handle to hit the man over the head.

The driver rolled onto his back and raised his arms to protect his face.

Lane released Randy and grabbed the shovel handle at the top of its arc. Christine turned on him, her face stained red with rage. "I hate assholes like him!"

Arthur said, "They're leaving."

Randy climbed into the passenger seat of the pickup. The driver slammed his door. The diesel engine wheezed and clattered as the driver reversed onto the boulevard. Brakes squealed as another driver avoided the Ford. The truck shifted into first. The diesel belched black smoke. The pickup sped away.

Lane looked around him. Matt brushed dirt and grass from his pants. Arthur looked at Christine as if seeing her in a very different way. She looked at each one of them in turn before she said, "I hate bullies."

"Uncles?" Matt said to Lane and Arthur. "You okay?"

"They're my uncles too, you know!" Christine moved toward Matt. Lane stepped in between.

"I don't have anybody else," Matt said.

"Neither do I." Christine began to cry. "What makes you think they're yours and not mine?"

"So, why didn't you call?" Erinn held a sleeping Jessica against her breast.

This entire argument is going to take place at a whisper, Harper thought. "Lane was wounded. We had to get him to the hospital, then I had to drive him to the Animal Shelter. It's way down south."

"How is he?" Erinn asked.

"On his feet. In as much trouble with Arthur as I am with you."

Jessica began to suck air in her sleep. Erinn adjusted her breast. Jessica sucked hungrily. "Still doesn't explain why you couldn't call me. I don't like getting the call from somebody else. I need to hear your voice and know you're okay."

"There wasn't one moment after the shooting started. Lane was wounded, I called it in, cruisers and an ambulance showed up. Everybody had a million questions." Harper touched his daughter's hair and wondered how she could be so beautiful and so soft.

"Call me next time. Call me right away." Erinn looked at the baby, then at her husband.

Harper saw the tears in her eyes. "I'm hoping there won't be a next time."

Shootings Shatter Calm

Two separate shooting incidents have resulted in one detective being wounded.

Detectives investigated reports of a shooting at an acreage owned by Blake Rogers on the western edge of the city limits.

When the detectives visited a second acreage, they were fired upon. One of the detectives was wounded and released late yesterday.

Blake Rogers said, "Things are getting out of control here. One of my friends is dead. Two others have disappeared. The police better get this thing under control before people start protecting themselves."

The name of the wounded detective has yet to be released.

chapter 8

"So the bullets from the weapon that wounded me don't match the ones from Blake Rogers' house?" Lane sat leaning on an elbow, keeping his weight on his left cheek while perched on the couch in his front room.

"The bullets from Blake's house were 7.62 by 39 millimetres. Fibre thinks they're from an AK-47. The bullet taken from …"

"My rear end?" Lane closed his eyes to feel the afternoon sun on his face. He'd finished the painkillers and was discovering a heightened appreciation for simple pleasures, especially ones that didn't involve pain.

"And the tire. It was a .22 calibre." Harper scrolled down the page of his laptop.

Christine and Matt were out walking the dog. Arthur was out getting last-minute groceries. Lisa, Loraine, Jessica, Erinn, and Glenn were on their way over for dinner.

"I'm just glad I was hit with the .22." Lane opened his eyes to see Harper smiling.

"I'm just glad we can joke about this." Harper turned back to the laptop. "Fibre found where both shooters fired from. He just measured the angles and walked in a straight line back along the trajectories. Both shooters wore cowboy boots. Neither left any shell casings. They had different shoe sizes. Eva's shooter had size twelves and Blake's wore tens."

"What about the broken glass at Blake's?" Lane looked out the window to see if the kids and dog were on their way home.

"That's where it gets interesting. Fibre thinks the shooter was standing with his feet together while aiming at a glass jar on top of the hay bale. Fibre thinks the recoil of the AK got away on the shooter. That would explain the climbing angle of the bullet holes and relatively equal spacing." Harper took a sip of water.

"Target practice?" Lane struggled to keep his mind clear of the aftereffects of pain killers.

"Looks like one possibility."

"And Eva's?"

Harper watched pain cross Lane's face. "You sure you want to do this today?"

"After fourteen hours of sleep, my mind's been racing, going over and over the events. Yes, I need to do this today."

"Sure it isn't the drugs?"

Lane smiled. "So, you heard about my mooning. I'd never taken that drug before. How was I to know I'd react like that? It was an unusual experience." He felt his face turning red.

"I see! The drugs made me do it!" Harper smiled. "The shooter at Eva's place was in a prone position. Fibre believes he was six feet tall. He was approximately one hundred and seven metres away at the edge of a clump of trees. The shooter took three shots and walked away. The foot trail ended at a gravel road." Harper hesitated for a moment. "I got the impression that the shooter made every shot he wanted to make."

"You mean he was aiming at me?"

"No, the damage to the bullet taken from you indicates it was a ricochet. Also, it was pretty nearly spent when it hit you. That's why the penetration was relatively shallow. What I'm talking about is the fact that he hit the gas tank twice and the rear tire once. You and I were at the front of the car behind the engine. It looks to me like he was trying to miss us."

Lane shifted his weight. "Somehow, that's not very comforting."

"This theory does explain the location of the initial impact point of all three bullets," Harper said.

"Actually, I've been thinking of something else."

"What's that?"

"The guy who came after us with the shovel handle. I've been thinking about that." Lane looked directly at Harper.

"But no one got a license plate number." Harper shook his head as if that would help him follow Lane's line of thinking.

"It's not that. It's the mark on Lombardi's back and the angle of the blow to the back of his head." Lane closed his eyes as he replayed the scene. "If the first blow caught him on the back and he fell to his knees, then the second blow would strike him exactly where it did on the back of the skull." Lane shuddered when he thought about what would have happened if he hadn't taken the handle away from Christine.

"You think that's how Lombardi died? Two blows like that?"

"It fits the evidence." Lane thought, *What do I do about Christine? She could have killed that guy.*

"There's one thing that doesn't fit." Harper said.

"What's that?"

Harper hesitated for a minute. "You said those two guys in the Ford knew you were gay almost right away."

"That's right."

Harper closed his laptop. "How did they know?"

The answer caught Lane by surprise. *It can't be that obvious.*

Harper read Lane's expression, "What?"

Lane scratched the stubble on his chin. "I don't know. Arthur's voice, I guess. Or ..."

"Or?"

Lane took a breath and exhaled. "It's so damned obvious. Two guys in a pickup truck. Four city boys living in a ranch house. Big trucks. Macho lifestyles. Maybe we're missing what's right in front of our eyes. They're all trying to pass themselves off as straight men."

"How come you've already dismissed Eva as a suspect?" Harper asked.

"Lane?" Glenn sat with everyone else at the table on the deck at Arthur and Lane's house. "How's your wound healing up?"

Once again, Christine looked confused when she looked at Glenn. She'd met Harper's nephew for the first time. He had his hair tinged with red and wore matching white-gold earrings.

"It's one big bruise," Arthur said.

"Like your face." Matt pointed at Lane with a fork.

Lane looked at Lisa and smiled. She was watching the conversation with more than her usual interest. The six foot tall RCMP officer sat beside a petite blonde, her partner. Loraine studied Christine and her reactions to all that was happening around her. Lane thought, *That's just like Loraine. She's always the psychologist; right now she's analyzing Christine, the newest member of the group.*

"So," Glenn smiled at Lane, "do we have to go to the Animal Shelter to get a look at your scar?"

Erinn almost choked on a sip of cranberry juice. "Glenn!" Then she laughed despite her disapproval.

Arthur held the baby. Jessica sat in the crook of his arm with her eyes watching the people at the table. She developed a gradual, then total interest in her thumb.

"That's not something I want to see again!" Matt was in a mood not to be outdone by Glenn, who was at least as quick-witted.

"Let's see." Glenn rolled his eyes. "How does one explain away a wound like that? A macho man would say it was a war wound. Mild-mannered would call it a bummer. An obscene person would call it being rear-ended. I would call it a blast in the—"

"Glenn!" Erinn tried to be stern while giggling.

"*Ass* far as that goes, we could say, in the end it was just a slap on the backside!" Matt sat back with a self-satisfied grin.

"It's not funny." Christine got up from the table and started to pick up dishes. "He could have been killed! It was just lucky that the bullet hit him there instead of somewhere else."

Matt laughed. "Yes, a few centimetres one way or the other and he could have been—"

"Shut up! Can't you see how serious this is?" Christine glared at Matt. "You're such a jerk."

Matt went to reply and closed his mouth. His face turned red.

Erinn caught Lane's eye and mouthed the words, "Talk to her."

Loraine watched Christine's reaction with clinical interest.

Lisa seemed unable to keep her eyes off Jessica. "Come on Arthur, it's my turn to hold her."

"It's time to retire to the living room. Christine and I will take care of the dishes." Lane got up slowly. He was aching in places he hadn't expected to ache: his back, shoulders, arms, and neck.

"I'll help." Harper stood with his plate. Erinn grabbed his arm and shook her head.

Lane ran the water in the sink and worked next to Christine as they loaded the dishwasher. Lane looked out the window. The dog scratched at the back door.

Christine went to open it.

"Wait a minute, please," Lane said.

"When are we gonna name the dog?" Christine asked.

"As soon as we agree on a name." Lane wiped the inside of the sink with a soapy washcloth.

"I don't like the way they joke about you getting shot." Christine closed the dishwasher and grabbed a tea towel.

"Nobody noticed." Lane smiled at his niece. "It's just their way of saying they're glad I'm okay. You know, sometimes you can't make up your mind whether to laugh or cry. So, you laugh."

"Oh." Christine leaned against the counter. "I just thought they were making fun of you."

"What else are you worried about?" Lane began to fill the sink with water and gave it a squirt of dish soap.

"I … well … How do I ask?" Christine's face turned red.

Lane began to scrub the inside of the pot. "Just say it."

"Loraine and Lisa, are they gay?"

"That's right." *I think I know where this is going,* Lane thought.

"Well, Loraine keeps looking at me." Christine took the pot from Lane and began to dry.

"She's a psychologist. You're the new person at the table, and she's figuring you out. She's very good at what she does." Lane realized his mistake too late.

"She thinks I'm crazy?"

"No. Loraine is a people watcher. That's what she does." *Think fast,* he thought. "And no, Loraine's not trying to pick you up."

Christine's ears turned red. "This is all so different."

Lane put a salad bowl in the sink. "I wanted to talk with you about the other day."

"What do you mean?" Christine's defenses went up all over again.

"The guy you hit. It scared me. When I think back on it, the whole thing scares me." Lane wiped the inside of the bowl.

"If Matt hadn't flipped him the bird, none of it would have happened. He's such a hothead!" She crossed her arms.

"If I had to do it over again, there are a few things I would change. The thing that's worrying me now is the wooden handle." Lane rinsed the bowl and handed it to Christine.

"What about it?" She wiped the bowl with her towel.

"What set you off?" Lane looked at his niece.

"It was what the driver said."

"Well?" Lane pulled a platter from the counter and started to wash it.

"He told you, 'God doesn't like people like you or her for that matter.' That's the kind of thing Whitemore said in church every week for six months before I left. He'd stand up there, look down on me and say, 'God spoke to me. I had a vision. He said that we must be vigilant. He told us that homosexuality and sexual intercourse with the negro is against God's law. God knows those who break this law will have no place in Paradise.' He said 'God knows' so often, I can hear him saying it now. He wanted me to leave. And when he started saying I should leave, that's when it got nasty."

"What do you mean?" Lane thought, *Maybe this isn't the time to tell her that Eva thinks I had a vision.*

"I'd turn my back and someone would bump into me. Leaving church, after one of his sermons, I'd get elbowed in the ribs. Half the time, I couldn't tell who did it. And no one, not even my mother, said anything. I had bruises on top of bruises." Christine took the wet platter from Lane.

"I'm sorry."

"For what? You didn't do anything." She held the platter and let the water drip into the sink.

Lane kept his hands in the soapy water, fishing for a fork. "That's the problem, I didn't do anything. I listened to what some other people had to say. They believed I wasn't fit to be your uncle. By the time I realized they were wrong, it was too late. You and your mother had disappeared."

Christine was silent for a moment. "That's really the way you feel?"

"Yes."

"Maybe we both listened to the wrong people." Christine rubbed Lane's back then pulled her hand away, leaving a wet mark on his shirt. "Does that hurt?"

He smiled. "Right now, almost everything hurts. Still, it's good to have you around again."

Christine looked at him. "You mean that?"

"Of course I do."

After the dishes, they sat down in the living room. Glenn, Christine, and Matt took the dog for a walk.

Erinn looked at the way Arthur sat contented with the sleeping baby. "Arthur? Why won't Lane see the police shrink?"

Arthur looked at Erinn. Conversation died while everyone in the room focused on his answer. "His family sent him to a shrink when he came out. The psychiatrist was a member of the church. He tried to convince Lane that he was making a choice to be gay. That he needed to be deprogrammed."

Lane followed the conversation, at the same time

thinking about his blood soaking through Eva's tea towel as he sat with Harper on the grass next to her house.

"But, last year Lane worked with Loraine and she's a psychologist. That was no problem," Harper said.

"That's different. He knew Loraine before and besides, he trusts her." Arthur looked at Harper. "Like he trusts you."

Lisa got up and held out her hands.

"Okay. Okay." Arthur handed her the sleeping baby.

Lisa lifted Jessica, tucked her in the crook of her arm, and sat back down next to Loraine.

Loraine smiled, looked at the detectives and asked, "How are you two feeling about the shooting?"

Harper looked at Lane, who said, "You first."

"I'm having flashbacks about the first time I was shot." Harper looked at Erinn. She stared back at him with an intensity that forced him to look away.

"The first time?" Loraine asked.

Harper took a long breath. "It was a leg wound."

"And you?" Loraine turned to Lane.

"Right now, my mind keeps going over the events, trying to figure out what happened. It happened so fast; it's confusing." Lane looked at the faces watching him.

Erinn said, "We've just had a baby and I'm worried. Whenever I think about what could have happened, I think I'm going to go crazy!"

Harper put his hand on Erinn's.

"I've been doing some reading and your reactions are pretty typical. Events like this leave a scar. It's when the people affected start to shut down or act out in atypical ways that you have to be careful." Loraine smiled. "We'll say that the mooning incident at the Animal Shelter was drug induced. Or we could say that it's the first indication of a much larger problem!"

Lane laughed. Jessica was startled awake and began to cry. Lisa stood and rocked the baby. Jessica's eyes closed. Her fists opened as she relaxed.

Harper watched with interest. "You've got the knack."

Lisa looked pleased with herself. She sat down. "Actually," Lisa looked at Loraine who nodded, "we've got an announcement of our own. We're expecting."

Everyone looked at Loraine.

Loraine turned to Lisa.

"How come everyone thinks it's Loraine? I'm thirteen weeks pregnant." Lisa's eyes filled with tears. "Sorry. Everyone we've told has reacted the same way. Can't see me as the motherly type, I guess. And my hormones are running wild." She wiped at her eyes.

The front door opened. The dog rushed in. She went immediately to Lisa. The dog put her chin on Lisa's knee.

Glenn was next in the room. "Hey, we've got two new choices for the dog's name. Do you want to vote?"

Christine and Matt stood on either side of Glenn.

"We can't decide," Glenn said. "It's either Babs or Wilde."

Matt pointed a thumb at Glenn. "His idea."

"Neither one of the names makes any sense." Christine shook her head and frowned.

"You know, Streisand; Babs. Wilde; Oscar Wilde," Glenn said.

"Wilde is a boy's name?" Christine asked.

"Roz. That dog's a Roz if ever I saw one," Erinn said. "Now, that's settled. After I feed Jessica, we need to figure out how to get us all to the rodeo."

If anyone else had said it, Lane thought, *it would have been dismissed out of hand, but because Erinn said it with just the right amount of confidence and enthusiasm, the name stuck.*

Fifteen minutes later, Harper and Lane sat with Lisa and Loraine on the deck. Inside, Erinn fed Jessica while chatting with Christine and Arthur. Matt and Glenn were at the kitchen table deep in their own conversation.

"We were hoping you could give us some background on the Alex Starchild case." Lane sipped wine and looked through the glass at Lisa.

Harper played with the cap from his bottle of beer.

Lisa sipped a glass of ice water. "There was an extensive investigation. The problem there was the lack of evidence. The eyewitness could not positively identify the truck's license plate. She didn't see the occupants of the vehicle. Aidan, I believe her name was, did remember seeing a front plate with 'Republic of Alberta' on it. Investigating officers checked pickups of the same colour in the area, but there was no consistent body damage on any of them."

Harper pushed the pop can away. "Were there any promising suspects?"

"We kept getting calls from people in the area who wanted the investigators to take a closer look at a guy named Blake Rogers, but there was no physical evidence to link him to the boy who was killed." Lisa sat up in her chair.

"Did you do any of the interviewing?" Lane asked.

Lisa shook her head. "The guys investigating the crime kept digging and kept coming up empty. I read over the reports."

"That's it, then?" Loraine asked.

"Unless there's new information," Lane said.

"Actually, there is something else." Harper leaned forward and looked directly at Loraine. "Lane won't go near downtown anymore. Since the fire, he's come to fewer and fewer meetings. He's been downtown maybe once or twice this month. The staff sergeant is asking questions. To make matters worse, it looks like the chief is getting ready to retire. Deputy Chief Calvin Smoke's makin' his move. He figures he's got a shot at becoming the top dog. He's backed by all of his friends in the scotch drinkers' club."

Lane glared at Harper, who ignored him.

"Scotch drinkers' club?" Loraine asked.

Harper shook his head. "Bunch of cops who meet once a month to drink expensive scotch, pat each other on the back, network. Get the picture?"

Lisa said, "Otherwise known as a misogynists' club?"

Harper pointed a finger and a beer bottle at Lisa. "You got it. Anyway, guess who's a member of the club?"

Lisa shrugged. Loraine shook her head.

"Stockwell," Lane said.

"And that's why you won't go downtown anymore?" Loraine asked.

Lane took a breath. "I thought we were moving forward, away from the old days. Now it looks like we're going back to the nineteen fifties. You know, the good old days when men were men and women were glad? Where the closet was closed and locked."

"Oh, I see," Loraine said without sounding convinced.

"How's staying away gonna make it any better?" Harper asked.

SATURDAY, JULY 6

ch*a*pter 9

"You know we have to go back out there," Harper said. They sat in Kuldeep's coffee shop on the west side of town. Harper wore his jacket and tie.

Lane wore a loose-fitting shirt and a pair of black sweatpants.

Fear gripped Lane. It was an oddly familiar sensation. "This is what you went through after you were shot?"

Harper took a breath. "Yep."

"And you're going through it again?" Lane took his cup of coffee in two hands.

Harper nodded. "The flashbacks started last night. One shooting gets all mixed up with the other. I keep hearing the ricochet, then the sound of the bullet smacking into flesh. When I look down, there's smoke coming out of my leg. It's weird."

"In my nightmare, I look down and see the blood soaking through my pants. Then I look around and there are hummingbirds circling the yard. I still can't figure out why I didn't feel pain until I saw the wound." Lane put his coffee down when the tremors started in his wrists and moved to his fingers.

"That's why we need to go back. We need to get the monkey off our backs and we need to talk to Eva." Harper thought, *Since you won't see the shrink, I'm gonna pass on what I learned the first time around, after I was wounded.*

"What about?" Lane asked.

"I did some checking this morning. You know, an electronic search using Eva's name. She filed a land claim about six months before Alex was killed." Harper opened up his laptop.

"Just tell me." Lane tried another sip of coffee to check if his hands were getting steadier.

"The basis of her claim is that the land she owns was originally reserve land. Later, it was given to an Anglican minister who had worked in the area for over twenty-five years. It was a kind of retirement gift for him. The problem was, no one from the First Nations was in on the land deal and the minister's land was originally part of the area covered by the treaty."

"And?"

Harper closed his laptop. "Eva bought her piece of land. It borders the T'suu T'ina Reserve, a proposed new development and other acreages. Some of her neighbours to the north and west could subdivide their land tomorrow and make huge profits. The problem is that Eva's land, and the land in question, is in the middle of the next stage of development. Makes investors reluctant to jump in when they might not see a return for a decade or more. It's even possible they might end up losing the land."

"So we may be talking about a motive for Alex's murder?" Lane asked.

"That, or at the very least, a reason for resentment between Eva and some of the other landowners. When you take a look at Blake Rogers' land, it gets even more interesting. He inherited the place from his grandmother. I checked into it, and the sale of similar properties. If Blake sold it today, he'd make millions."

"Why doesn't he sell, then?" Lane looked at Roz, who sat patiently outside on the other side of the coffee shop's glass wall. She raised her eyebrows hopefully. Roz and Lane had taken a slow walk to Kuldeep's to meet with Harper.

"Hey guys, want more coffee?" Kuldeep stood behind the counter with a smile and tired eyes from working fourteen-hour days, seven days a week.

"Maybe in a minute, thanks." Lane smiled back.

"No problem," Kuldeep said.

"I checked with a real estate friend. He said the cheaper properties are being bought up, but the land in Blake's price range isn't selling as well because investors who are willing to wait out the land claim — Who would want to sit on that kind of money? — are a little hard to come by. And, Blake's land is part of the land Eva is claiming rightfully belongs to the T'suu T'ina Nation." Harper leaned back and waited for Lane to get the picture.

"So we need to go and see Blake too?" Lane drained his coffee. He looked outside. Roz was on her belly with her head between her paws, staring at him with pleading brown eyes.

"There's more. After Alex died, Eva changed her will. The land will be passed on to an Aidan Walker and Eva's estranged daughter. Aidan was with Alex when he was killed."

"So, with an eyewitness, why hasn't this case been solved?" Lane stood up, grimaced, and took his cup over to Kuldeep. "One for me and another for him, please." He pulled out a twenty dollar bill.

"No problem." Kuldeep smiled.

"How are you doing?" Lane asked.

"This franchise has made a slave of me. Besides that, everything is good." She filled their cups.

"What do you mean slave?" Lane asked.

"The way it works is that the company from Toronto takes its money out of my bank account every month. There's not much left after the rent is paid and the company is finished with me. They made a lot of big promises about how much money I would make and their promises turned out to be wrong." Kuldeep smiled as she passed over the coffees.

"I don't understand. You should be able to make a living and it's always busy here."

Kuldeep shrugged. "As long as we're open and paying taxes, the company in Toronto is making money and the company does whatever it wants. No one, including the government, wants to hear about how I've become a slave to the franchise because there's not enough money left at the end of the month to pay a living wage."

Lane returned to the table and took his time sitting down.

Harper pulled his fresh cup closer. "When Alex was killed, the crime happened outside of the city limits. Now the land is inside the city. The RCMP had a few suspects, but Aidan didn't see the rear license plate. She only saw the front plate and couldn't say exactly who was in the truck." Harper got up to add cream and sugar to his coffee.

Lane waited until Harper got back. "Republic of Alberta?"

"Yep. The RCMP tracked down several pickups matching the vehicle description. Blake Rogers was a person of interest. His vehicle was suspicious, because he lives nearby. It looked like the truck had two new doors, but the RCMP couldn't get anyone to talk. And they couldn't find any damage to the vehicle, or blood, hair, or tissue evidence to connect the vehicle to Alex Starchild."

"So, who exactly is this Aidan Walker?" Lane talked louder as Kuldeep steamed coffee.

"I met her while you were in the sweat lodge." Harper looked out the window at Roz. "She's some kind of artist or puppeteer."

"That's all we know?" Lane asked.

"So far." Harper stared at his reflection in the window.

Lane saw the far off look in his partner's eyes. "Another flashback?"

Harper turned back to Lane. "How did you know?"

Aidan wore a short gold skirt made full with layers of underlying crinoline. Under the skirt, she wore black spandex pants and black running shoes. Her blue, tight-fitting jacket was pinstriped and accented with a white silk tie. Her blonde hair was combed back. As always, her marionette persona was dressed the same way.

"It sucks." Alex sat in a chair under the catwalk with his legs stretched out front.

"You're not going to complain about your costume again, are you?" Aidan, the marionette, stood over him.

"Now that you mention it…." Alex stood up and smiled. "Actually, I was going to say it sucks that you don't have a life."

"What do you mean?" Aidan crossed her arms.

"I'm your only friend. A dead friend at that. And Eva is your family. The fact is, Eva's getting old. Once she's gone, there will only be me. Now, as much as I love being around you, a warm body would be a lot better for you. Just because your parents left you behind and moved to Australia for a stupid job doesn't mean you can't trust anyone but me and Eva." Alex put a hand on Aidan's shoulder.

Aidan pushed the hand away. "I'm not ready for that. You never understood that. When your parents do that to you, it shows you what they really value."

"So, you moved in with me and Eva." He leaned forward in his chair.

"You're family. More than my parents are. And, since you're asking, I'm doing okay," Aidan said.

"Well you'd better start meeting other people. The way people have been disappearing around the old homestead, it looks like warm bodies will be at a premium. Now that a cop's been shot, things could get even more dangerous." Alex walked away from Aidan.

"Things will cool down. They always do. What they did to you has to be settled. I made a promise to you and myself that the guys who killed you would end up facing what they did." Aidan followed Alex off stage.

Alex said, "But what happens to you and your life? You like to start fires, get people going. What's that say about you?"

"That I've waited long enough for the police to do their jobs, and now I'm doing what I can to settle this thing."

"What if it gets worse? You know as well as I that people are talking about barricading the highway. Some hotheads want to stop the city from getting any closer," Alex said.

"What are they fighting about?" Arthur leaned on an elbow to look at the bedside clock.

Lane opened his eyes. "What time is it?"

"One AM." Arthur heaved himself out of bed.

Lane rolled over, saw light along the bottom of the door and thought, *The hallway light is on*. He recalled a three dimensional dream, compliments of the painkiller he'd taken before bed. It had something to do with falling off a bridge into fast-moving water the colour of eye shadow.

"She's sleeping with *me*!" Christine said.

"Stay out of here you bitch! Roz is sleeping in *my* room!" Matt said.

"That's no way to talk to me!" Christine pounded

on Matt's door, then ran upstairs with Matt close behind.

Lane thought, *I wonder when she'll learn how to swear? If she doesn't, it's going to start costing a fortune in doors.*

Arthur opened the door. "What's going on, you two?"

Lane saw the forest of hair on Arthur's back and backside. He was framed in the door and illuminated by the hallway light.

Christine screamed and ran into her bedroom.

Matt looked at Roz and then back at Arthur. Matt's eyes lit up. "It's Uncle Wrinkly!"

Arthur stepped back inside and closed the door.

In the darkness, Lane heard an exasperated Arthur say, "I handled that very well, don't you think?"

"At least you stopped the fight," Lane said.

Water Fever

Local grocery stores and fresh water suppliers are scrambling to meet the demand for drinking water. Three major grocery chains have sold out of all brands of bottled water.

A spokesperson for Safeway explained, "We have been unable to keep up with the demand for our bottled waters. At present, we are nearly sold out of soft drinks."

One shopper explained, "When I found out about the body in the reservoir and those two missing fellows, I didn't want to risk drinking from the tap."

chapter 10

The Chev's tires rumbled over the country road. Gravel ricocheted against the underside of the car. Lane's stomach lurched as they crested a hill and experienced momentary weightlessness.

"So what did you think of the medical examiner's report on Lombardi's cause of death?" Harper drove.

And he can't stop talking, Lane thought, *He must be as scared as I am.* "What did *you* think?" Lane thought, *If he needs to talk, then let him talk.* Lane tried shifting his weight to find a more comfortable position. *The pain will happen. It's the expectation of pain, that's the killer.*

"I think he's right about the two blows that killed Lombardi. It makes sense. One to the back between the shoulder blades. The next to the back of the head. That's the one that finished him. Just like you said it would. Dead long before he hit the river. No evidence of drowning. Oh, and Erinn told me to say thanks for dinner. She likes Christine. Erinn figures things will eventually settle down between Christine and Matt. Says she thinks the girl's all mixed up because of the cult thing. It's a cult, isn't it?"

"That's a good question." *What religion isn't?* Lane thought. He looked right, to the mountains. The morning light appeared to bring the peaks closer. He longed to drive a long mountain valley highway with nothing to think about except whether he'd see a bear or a wolf.

"How come you're back to work today? I mean, you should have taken a couple of weeks off."

Lane thought for a minute while he leaned his right cheek off the seat. The car hit a valley in the road. He wanted to say, "If I don't do this now, I might never go back." Out loud, he said, "Just doing what you suggested!" He thought, *Why are you taking it out on Harper?* "You ready for this?"

"Nope. And Erinn wanted to apologize for putting in her two cents about the dog's name. She felt like she might have upset Matt."

"It's okay." Now Lane understood why Matt was so angry the other night. Christine liked the name Roz but none of the ones Matt suggested. *Every single decision becomes so damned complicated,* he thought.

"We're here." Harper allowed the Chev to coast and decelerate. "We're still going to the rodeo, aren't we?"

"It'll be fun." As they turned into Eva's driveway, Lane studied the surrounding terrain for anything that looked out of place.

Harper watched ahead and to the left.

Lane's eyes scanned the right. His hand moved closer to his Glock.

They parked beyond the blackened patch of driveway where their other car had burned. Lane stepped out of the Chev before the engine quit. As his eyes scanned the perimeter, he couldn't escape the feeling that his back was unprotected.

Eva stepped out from behind a hedge.

The engine stopped. Harper climbed out of the car.

Lane felt the cool, morning mountain air. He saw that Harper was sweating, his eyes never stopping on one thing for more than a fraction of a second. Harper's hand was close to his pistol.

Eva wore a white hand-knit sweater over a dress with a pattern of spring flowers on a blue background. She moved toward Harper. "Come inside. Coffee's on. Muffins in the oven." They followed her along the sidewalk leading to the back door. Inside, as they took their shoes off, Eva said, "Don't wanna hear no jokes about smoke signals."

"What?" Lane waited for Eva to go up the stairs.

Eva turned to him. She smelled of sage from this morning's smudge. "Hearin' lots of jokes about me sending up smoke signals the other day. People talkin', callin' and tellin' me to use the phone like everybody else."

"Oh." Harper covered his mouth with his hand to hide a smile.

They followed Eva upstairs and sat at the kitchen table. Eva brought coffee and muffins. They sat on three sides of the table, with the sound of spoons clinking against the sides of coffee cups.

"This real cream?" Harper asked.

Eva nodded.

They waited for at least five minutes while Harper ate muffins, Lane tried unsuccessfully to get comfortable, and Eva watched them through the steam from her coffee.

"You okay?" Eva looked through the fog at Lane.

"Better." Lane looked back at Eva and tried to smile.

"You?" Eva looked at Harper.

"Okay." Harper spoke out of the side of a mouth filled with muffin.

"Got kids?" Eva looked at Harper first.

"A baby and a nephew. Jessica's four months old and Glenn is eighteen."

"You?" Eva looked at Lane.

"Ahhh," Lane said.

"He's got a nephew, Matt, who's sixteen and a niece, Christine. She's seventeen. They arrived on his doorstep with their clothes and little else," Harper said.

"Throwaway kids?" Eva put her coffee down.

"What?" Lane asked.

"Kids get kicked out of home. They gotta be somewhere." Eva waited for one of them to reply.

Lane thought, *I don't know where this is going. She'll know if I'm hiding. And I'm getting tired of hiding or maybe just tired from lack of sleep.* "Matt is my partner's nephew. Matt's mom died of cancer. His dad started a new family. Matt has CP and his dad wants a perfect son. Now he's got one and we've got Matt. My niece is running from Paradise. Have you heard of it?"

Eva nodded. "You're gay?"

Lane nodded. He waited for comment, half expecting recrimination, judgement, or rejection from Eva, but sensing instead a simple acceptance of the facts of his life.

"You?" Eva looked at Harper.

"My nephew, Glenn, was kicked out of his house and came to live with us." Harper looked back at Eva with curiosity. "Jessica's our first child, or second depending on how you look at it."

He's wondering where this conversation will end up, Lane thought. *And so am I.*

Eva looked out the window when she spoke. "Alex was my daughter's son. She's thirty-five now. Last time I heard from her, she was in the States. Alex was with me for fourteen years." Eva looked at Lane. "Alex was gay too." She looked down at her coffee. "Aidan's gonna stay here after I'm gone. Maybe someday my daughter'll decide to come home. That way, there'll be a place for her. Been a long time since I saw my daughter. So much is different now.

"When I was young, we used to walk along the road into the city. We could always get a lift. Had to keep our eyes open, though. Sometimes drivers would open their doors and try to knock us over. Thought those days were over. Didn't teach Alex to keep his eyes open.

"Imagine losing a child like that." Eva took a sip of coffee. "After Alex died, Aidan stayed. Now it feels like she's my family. Her parents moved to Australia. Aidan needed a place to stay. Likes it here. Told me she feels accepted. She still talks with Alex. Thinks I don't know, but I do. It's like she can't let go of him, or he can't let go of her. They were so close and then somebody opened his truck door. That's why these shootings are happening. Times haven't changed that much. People have no right to run down children like that. If it was your child, would you ever forget?" Eva looked at each of them in turn. "Don't know who took those boys away from Blake's place. Don't know why that one boy was in the river. Don't know who shot at Blake. Just know that it's because of what happened to Alex. And, there's a lot of people around here fed up with the whole mess. There's even talk of a barricade."

Footsteps climbed up the stairs to the back door. It opened. "Eva? It's me."

Lane and Harper stood.

Eva smiled at the detectives. "Don't worry."

"You okay, Eva? They takin' you to jail?" Norm asked.

"Nope." Eva stood and went to the stairs. "Coffee?"

"Okay." Norm topped the stairs dressed in a green work shirt, pants, and a yellow ball cap. He looked at Harper. "Hi."

Harper got up and shook hands with Norm. "How are you?"

"Fine." Norm kept his eyes away from Lane. "Came to help get the teepee ready for Stampede."

"Sit down," Eva said.

Norm sat at the table and Eva brought him a cup of coffee. She topped up the other three cups as well.

Harper said, "This is Detective Lane."

"Hello." Lane held out his hand.

"Gonna put the cuffs on me?" Norm kept his hands under the table.

"No," Eva said. "We're talkin' is all."

Norm nodded. "See the news today?"

Lane and Harper looked at one another.

Eva said, "What happened?"

"All those city people buyin' up bottled water. They think there's bodies in the reservoir. Stores are sold out of the stuff." Norm smiled at the idea. "City people are always worryin' about the wrong things."

"People are scared," Eva said.

Norm added three teaspoons of sugar and filled the cup to the brim with cream. He slid the cup nearer to the edge of the table, leaned over and slurped. He raised his head. "Good coffee." He looked around the table with mischief in his eyes. "Water from the reservoir?"

Eva laughed. "Nope."

Norm looked at Lane. "You the party that was shot a couple of days ago?"

"That's right," Lane said.

"Eva had nothin' to do with it." Norm picked up his coffee and drank with his eyes on Lane.

"I didn't think she was involved." Lane looked at Eva, who watched Norm.

"How do you know?" Harper asked Norm.

"Keep my ear close to the ground. See what's going on, you know." Norm reached for a muffin.

"Who did the shooting?" Lane asked.

"The one at the Rogers' place?" Norm picked up a muffin and broke it in two with callused fingers.

"The one here." Harper studied Norm's face.

"Not sayin'." Norm stuck the muffin in his mouth.

"How come?" Lane asked.

Norm shrugged and mimed pulling a zipper across his lips.

Lane thought, *I'd better change my approach and quickly.* "At the Rogers' place?"

"Bet Blake did it his self." Norm spit bits of muffin as he spoke.

"How?" Lane kept an even tone of voice and spoke just above a whisper.

"Doesn't know one end of a gun from the other." Norm washed the muffin down with half a cup of coffee. He looked at Eva. "Gotta get the teepee up and checked out. Stampede's almost here."

Eva looked at the detectives. "We live at the village during Stampede. It's like a holiday."

"Indian village?" Harper asked.

Eva looked directly at him. "First Nations!"

"What did I do wrong? She just clammed up." Harper drove west from Eva's.

"Not sure. Whatever it was, it made a promising conversation stop dead in its tracks." Lane thought, *Maybe that was what she wanted.*

"Sorry."

"Maybe she wasn't mad."

"What do you mean?" Harper glanced at Lane.

"Maybe she didn't like the direction the conversation was going, so she pretended to be offended."

"How do you know?" Harper slowed to turn left.

"Something she said in between rounds at the sweat lodge. 'The words aren't as important as what's in your heart when you say them.' Maybe she was trying to protect Norm."

"Why would she need to do that?" Harper asked as they neared Blake's acreage.

"That's another question we'll need to find an answer to. But first, we have to ask Blake a few questions."

Harper parked near the black pickup truck. Again, they took a good look around before Harper turned the engine off. Blake opened the front door when Lane knocked.

"You find out who shot up my house?" Blake held a long-necked beer bottle in his right hand.

"Perhaps." Lane looked directly at Blake.

"That's good news." Blake took a pull on the beer

but didn't invite them in. With his free hand, he gently touched his gelled hair to ensure it was perfect.

"The evidence suggests that someone was doing target practice at the back of your house. The shattered glass near the hay bails, the stance of the shooter, and the rising pattern of the bullet holes along the house all indicate this. Someone unfamiliar with the recoil of an AK-47 would find that the weapon tends to run away if the shooter isn't prepared for it." Lane paused and waited for a reaction from Blake.

Blake smiled. He hooked his free thumb behind his belt buckle.

Harper said, "Also, when houses are shot at, shooters often aim for windows, not for siding and the roof."

Blake's smile faded. "So what are you sayin'?"

Harper and Lane waited.

"You're sayin' I shot up my own place?" Blake looked over his shoulder as if measuring the distance to something hidden inside.

"Actually, we didn't say it. You did." Harper took a step forward.

"Assholes! Somebody shoots up my place, and you come here to say I did it!" Blake pointed at his chest with the beer bottle. Beer spilled down the front of his shirt.

"Did Rosco come home?" Lane asked.

Blake stepped back inside and slammed the door.

When they were back in the car, Harper said, "Sure touchy about that dog, isn't he?"

Aidan wore her short gold shorts, black spandex tights and blue jacket. This time she wore a blue ball cap. The marionettes, Aidan and Alex, were suspended below her, already in conversation.

"So, the show's nearly ready to go." Alex pretended to wipe sweat from his forehead.

Aidan looked at her toes. "We have to do the death scene soon."

"Great. I've been looking forward to this! I've got it all planned out." Alex stepped back a few paces. He turned to face Aidan. "I'll stand here, and after the truck hits me, I'll throw my arms wide like I'm being crucified."

Aidan lifted her head. "You're such a drama queen! Isn't anything sacred to you?"

Alex dropped his arms. "You mean like life, family, politics, and religion?" He made the sign of the cross.

"Yes, something like that." Aidan stood with her feet apart and her arms crossed.

"Well, *your* life is sacred but *mine* isn't. I live through you, remember?"

"It's hard to forget."

"As far as politicians go, the Premier called me 'victim of the week'. That left a bad taste in my mouth when it comes to politics. How could anyone be that thoughtless, that stupid? You think he'd been drinking again?" Alex adopted a thoughtful pose with his hand under his chin.

"What about religion?"

Alex laughed. "I'm an abomination in the eyes of most religions. He bent at the waist and smacked his backside. I'm deaf, aboriginal, and gay. My own minority group! I'm the poster boy for the fight for equal rights, and I'm First Nations! That means I'm the first to get screwed!" He galloped around the stage, slapping his flank.

"So where do we go from here?" Aidan looked worried.

"We do the show, of course. You put us on the stage and see what happens! Just don't blame me if it blows up in your face!"

"You really think anything bad can happen to a drag king?" Aidan fluttered her eyelashes. "Think the crowd might be offended by my wardrobe, my sense of style?"

"It won't be because of the way you dress. It'll be because you're still alive. You're still vulnerable. What can they do to me that hasn't already been done?" Alex leaned back and began to laugh.

"Where are the kids?" Lane bent over to pick up Roz's poop in the back yard.

Arthur grabbed a turd on the other side of the yard. "They took the dog for a walk."

"That's the last of it for now." Lane peeled the bag off his hand, dropped it into the bag of crap and tied it off.

Both dropped their loads over the fence and into the garbage can.

They looked across the street and saw Matt, dragged by a wheezing Roz and followed by Christine.

"I'm telling you she's just trying to recruit you. She's climbing the ladder to heaven. You're just another rung!" Christine said.

"Why do you have to be such a bitch?" Matt hurried ahead of her.

"I'm just telling you the truth!" Christine jogged to catch up. "You'll go to the dance, and she'll bring it up somehow. It'll go something like, 'Don't you want to go to heaven?' One of those questions you're only supposed to answer one way. Just see what happens if you say you're not interested."

"Maybe she just likes to dance." Matt crossed the road.

Lane looked at Arthur.

Arthur said, "Matt's got a date?"

MONDAY, JULY 8

chapter 11

"I don't see a problem," Lane said to Harper as he paid for the coffee. He handed his card to Kuldeep. She stamped it with a red coffee bean. "How's things?"

Kuldeep shook her head. "Still working. Still looking for a way out of the franchise."

Lane felt a surge of guilt. "What can I do?"

Kuldeep shrugged. "I don't know. Listen when I complain?" She tried to smile. "When I was a kid in India, my grandfather used to explain how London's colonial system worked. Nowadays it's called a franchise system run out of Toronto." She patted Lane's arm. "I'll bring your coffee over, guys."

Harper and Lane said, "Thanks," in stereo.

They found a table near the window, away from anyone who might overhear.

Harper continued the initial conversation. "The

roblem is, Sophia Lombardi just lost her brother and she made herself pretty clear last time we talked with her." He tapped the table with his index finger for emphasis.

"Yes and she's had time to think about what happened. There may be more she can tell us about her brother. After all, brothers and sisters are often more likely to confide in one another. Even Matt is starting to confide in Christine."

"I thought they hated one another." Harper looked over his shoulder to see if the first coffee of the day was on its way.

"That's what I thought at first, but they've been acting odd lately."

Harper looked out the window. "Odd how?"

"It's like they're becoming …" Lane searched his mind for the right word.

The door opened. Harper sized up the couple who walked in. He studied their hands, the way they took in the room. "Siblings?"

"That's it." Lane kicked Harper in the shin.

"What was that for?" Harper rubbed his leg.

"It's not likely we'll get shot at in here. Quit looking at people like they're armed." Lane leaned the weight of off his bruised cheek and winced at the pain from his wound.

"You just never know." Harper turned as Kuldeep brought their coffees.

"Here you go, guys," she said.

"Thanks," they said.

Lane closed his eyes, inhaling the scent of coffee and chocolate.

"So you want me to call Sophia Lombardi?"

Lane opened his eyes. "And we need to see her right away, before she has time to prepare any answers in her head."

It took only twenty minutes to get downtown and another hour to track Sophia down. They were told to look for her in The Diner. It was located on Stephen's Avenue Mall, where breakfast was served all day. The restaurant was somewhere between three and four metres wide, so Harper was forced to follow a couple of steps behind Lane. They passed a row of red metal tractor seats on metal poles for customers who preferred to sit at the counter. Black and white photos lined the wall on the other side. He spotted Sophia's red hair at a table near the back, next to the kitchen.

They stood in front of her as she read the newspaper. An unfinished cup of fresh fruit sat on the table alongside a half-empty cup of coffee. "Is it okay if we sit down?" Lane asked.

Sophia looked over the top of the paper.

Lane looked at her eyes. They had that numb-from-grief and lack-of-sleep look. She had been thin before; now her freckled face was beginning to look gaunt. Her face was free of makeup and her sunken cheeks appeared to be losing their tan.

Sophia's voice sounded empty when she said, "What now?"

"We have some questions we need to ask." Harper's voice was softer and quieter than usual.

She sighed. "Sit down."

Lane sat across from her. Harper pulled an adjacent table closer 'til it touched Sophia's.

"Have somethin' to eat." She glanced at the newspaper, then waved at the waitress. "One of the best places for breakfast in town."

"I'm not very hungry," Lane said.

"Too bad. You wanna talk, you gotta eat. These girls gotta make a livin' too. Can't make any money when people just sit and talk."

"I'll eat if you do." Lane thought, *There's no way we're going to get her out of here to a place more private. This is where it has to be.*

Sophia glared at him across the table as if to say, "I don't take shit from anyone, and especially not from you."

He watched her with obvious curiosity.

"You got balls." Sophia smiled. "When your food comes, I'll eat."

"What are you havin'?" The waitress poured coffee for each of them.

Lane noticed she wore black jeans and a black T-shirt. "Eggs over easy, bacon, and brown toast."

"Same," Harper said.

"Comin' up. Sophia, you okay?" the waitress asked.

Sophia looked up. The motion appeared to take a great deal of effort.

The waitress looked at Lane and Harper before looking back at Sophia. "You all right?"

"I'll let you know if I'm not." Sophia looked at Lane and Harper. "Jenn's an old friend."

Jenn took a long hard look at the detectives before leaving.

"We're hoping to talk with you about the relationship between Skip and Blake."

"They lived in the same house." Sophia looked back at Lane as if she were challenging him.

She wants to fight, Lane thought. *Any kind of distraction from the grief will do.* Lane waited.

"Duds was the reason my brother stayed there. After Duds disappeared, there was no reason for Skip to live there any longer." Sophia stared back at Lane.

Lane sensed her switch in mood from needing to fight to needing to talk. He said, "I'm not sure I understand."

"Duds and Skip were partners. Call it what you want. They loved each other. It's kind of hard for a rodeo rider to admit he's gay, if you know what I mean. That's why they didn't want to broadcast their relationship." Sophia's eyes narrowed. Her mouth was set in a straight line. "You two here to dig up dirt on my brother? You know, make it look like the 'fag' got what he deserved? That way you can say you solved the murder. It was just a queer spat. Nothing that regular people should worry about."

Harper shifted uncomfortably at the word 'fag'.

Lane looked at Harper as if to say, "Relax."

Jenn slid the plates onto the table. "Want ketchup and jam?"

"Please." Harper spoke between his teeth.

"How's it goin'?" Jenn asked Sophia.

Sophia shrugged.

"I can ask them to leave." Jenn put her fists on her hips. She looked toward the front of the restaurant, where a couple of beefy guys leaned their elbows on the counter.

Sophia looked from Lane to Harper, as if sizing them up again. "What's going on here?"

Lane decided it was time for everyone to come clean. "I'm gay. He's straight. I've got a partner; my niece just moved in. We also have a nephew and now a new dog at home." Lane pointed at Harper. "He's got a wife, new daughter, and nephew at his place. We're here to find out what we can about your brother and hopefully figure out who killed him."

Sophia sat back. She looked at Lane and Harper. She looked up at Jenn. "It'll be okay."

Jenn said, "Just wave if you need us."

"Can we eat?" Lane asked.

"Good idea," Sophia said.

They ate in silence, watching each other surreptitiously.

Jenn frequently returned under the pretext of re-filling their coffees. She took their plates away when they finished.

"You're right," Harper said.

"How's that?" Sophia said.

"The breakfast was great. Those fried potatoes are the best I've had in this city, or any other as far as that goes." Harper took a sip of coffee.

Sophia nodded. "I apologize."

"For what?" Lane asked.

"For usin' the 'f' bomb." Sophia leaned back against her seat. "I should never have used that word."

Lane shrugged. "It's not the word, it's the way it's used. You were defending your brother against a threat. Under the circumstances, I would have done the same thing."

"Skip and I were close," Sophia said.

"I gathered that." Lane decided to keep his responses as short as possible. *Let Sophia talk*, he thought.

"It wasn't easy for my brother. He thought my family would never accept his comin' out. Sure, my parents suspected, but we all let Skip play his macho game. You know, live in the country, hang around the rodeos. Live with four guys. Drive a pickup. Wear a cowboy hat. That kind of stuff." Sophia looked at the entrance to the restaurant as if expecting to see her brother walk through the door and wave at her when he saw her.

"We used to meet here for lunch at least once a week. This is where he told me what happened to the kid." Sophia looked at each of them in turn as if checking to see if they understood what she was talking about.

"Alex Starchild?" Lane asked.

"That's right. How much of this will end up in the papers?" Sophia asked.

Harper leaned forward. "We can't predict what the media will do with the story. We're looking for a killer, and we need evidence to arrest him."

"Or her," Sophia said.

Harper said, "Or her."

"Blake was drunk the day the kid was killed. He was always acting macho to pass. He thought if he acted like a redneck, no one would ever suspect he was gay. Skip used to joke about it. The day the kid was killed, they were drivin' home from the bar. Duds and Skip were in the back. Tyler was drivin'. Blake was up front, in the passenger seat. He spotted the kid in the ditch. Skip said that Blake screamed, 'Get that bastard!' Tyler steered to the edge of the road. Blake opened his door, braced it with his foot and the door hit the kid." Sophia's voice remained toneless. "Duds and Skip wanted to stop and check on the kid, but Blake told Tyler to keep goin'. Later on, Blake held the kid's death over their heads, especially after Tyler disappeared. Blake convinced them they'd all end up in jail if one of them talked. So, they kept quiet until Duds disappeared. Skip told Blake he was going to move out. That's what Skip and I were going to talk about that day, but he never turned up. Skip was going to move in with me until he could find a place of his own. And I think Skip was gettin' ready to talk to the cops."

"Any idea who killed your brother or what happened to the other two?" Lane asked.

"Blake always figured it was Eva. He figured it had something to do with her knowing who killed her grandson, the land claim or some other grudge she held against Blake's family. He would get drunk and just start ranting." Sophia sagged. "I feel responsible. If I'd just told the police this earlier, then my brother might still be alive."

Harper went to say something and stopped himself.

Lane shook his head at his partner. "Do you know what Blake did with the truck after he and Tyler ran Alex down?"

"Skip said he took it to some friend of his who fixed it. Paid ten thousand dollars for the guy to keep his mouth shut. At the time, Blake still had a plenty of his grandmother's inheritance." Sophia took a long breath.

"At the time?" Harper asked.

"Yeah. Blake's broke. Last time I saw him he was

bitchin' about havin' to go and look for a real job." Sophia's tone of voice was filled with venom.

"You hated him?" Lane asked.

Sophia looked surprised. "Don't you?"

"Think we have enough for a search?" Harper asked as they drove out of downtown following the southern banks of the Bow River. It was lunch hour. The joggers were out running two and three abreast along the pathway that lay between the road and the river.

"Enough at least for some more questions. It's always better to have some hard evidence to go along with a hearsay witness."

Twenty minutes later, they stopped just on the edge of the city for gas at the Super Service with its nineteen-fifties colours and geometric lines. Two men in black leather waited on their Harley motorcycles to cross the highway. In front of them, a woman in an electric wheelchair looked east and west. All three accelerated across the road and toward a new development about a half a kilometre away. "There's something you don't see everyday." Harper pulled up to the pumps, stepped out and began to fill the car with gas.

The attendant looked to be seventeen. She ran out and leaned on Lane's window. He saw black mascara tears running down her cheeks. She pushed back her black hair. "Glad you guys got here so fast. I only called, like, five minutes ago. It was pretty scary. I mean that guy on the motorcycle, he was going crazy. Saying he knew what that old lady was up to, and he was coming for her."

Lane held up his hand. "Whoa. Do you know the name of the old lady?"

"Eva. Everybody knows Eva. I went to school with Alex. Norm was in the truck with her." The young woman started to shake.

Lane said, "What's your name?"

"Kelsey. My family runs the station. Eva stopped for gas and a Slurpee. Norm loves his Slurpees. They paid for everything, and this guy pulled up on his motorcycle. You know, black helmet, black leather jacket and chaps. Black boots and dark sunglasses. Even the bike was black. Everybody around here knows who he is. Name is Blake.

"He started yelling at Eva. He said stuff like, 'You got my friends, but you're not gonna get me. Don't come near my place or I'll blow you away.' He kicked in the door of her truck, grabbed a squeegee and tried to smash her headlights. He acted like he was drunk. Eva had to stop Norm from going after Blake. I mean, Norm is a big, strong guy. Then a couple of cars full of people from T'suu T'ina pulled up. They saw what was going on and got out. There were about ten of them. Blake took off. The guys in the cars asked if Eva was okay, and I went inside to call you." Kelsey started to weep.

Harper finished filling up the car and returned the nozzle to the pump.

Lane got out of the car and glanced over the roof at his partner before turning back to Kelsey. "You said they left about five minutes ago?"

"That's right." Kelsey wiped her nose on her sleeve.

"We're going to pay for our gas, and then we're heading out to talk with Blake. Can you tell the officers, when they get here, that we're on our way to

Blake Rogers' place?" Lane took Kelsey back into the store.

"Okay," Kelsey said.

"You also need to call your family and let them know what happened," Lane said.

Kelsey nodded.

When Lane and Harper were back in the car, Lane called it in. After he finished, he looked at Harper. "The helicopter is on its way. All we have to do is block off Blake's driveway so he can't leave, then we'll wait for the helicopter and backup before going in."

Lane handled the calls and updates while Harper drove. When they turned off the pavement and onto the gravel road leading to Blake's acreage, they stopped to get their bulletproof vests out of the trunk.

"He may be impaired, and he may have an assault rifle." Lane took his jacket off before putting on a vest. He checked his pistol and extra magazines. He carefully laid his sports jacket in the trunk. *Usually my mind clears at times like this, but it's different this time. I can't get images of Matt and Christine out of my head.*

Harper waited with his hand on the open trunk lid. "Don't worry. We can't get shot at twice in a month. It just doesn't happen."

They got back in the car. Lane kept his window open and looked in the passenger mirror. The cloud of dust obscured the road behind them.

A call came in with an update; the police helicopter was three minutes away.

Harper slowed as they neared Blake's place. They saw a black motorcycle parked next to the black Ford pickup. Harper eased the Chev off the gravel road.

Lane saw Blake open the front door. He was still dressed in a leather jacket and matching black leather chaps. He held an assault rifle in his right hand.

"Gun!" Lane reached for his Glock.

Blake stepped onto the front step. He pulled back the bolt action on the automatic rifle.

Harper turned left. The Chev dove into a ditch that was more than a metre deep. The nose of the car rammed into the bottom of the ditch. Both air-bags deployed. The rear axle got hung up on the end of a section of corrugated-culvert pipe. Stunned by the impact of the airbag against the side of his head, Lane felt himself being dragged out of the car through Harper's door. Harper gripped the shoulder of Lane's vest and pulled him under the open door and around the front of the car.

Automatic rifle fire crashed over their heads.

"You hit?" Harper asked.

Lane lifted his Glock. "Not yet. Let's hope he still hasn't figured out how to use that weapon."

Bullets ripped into the trunk of the Chev.

Lane and Harper crouched as low as possible be-hind the grill and the engine.

"You bastards!" Blake screamed.

"Put down the gun!" Lane yelled back.

The answer was more automatic fire. The first two rounds hit the trunk and the rest zipped overhead.

Harper rolled left and crawled to the lip of the ditch. He fired two rounds into the pickup and rolled back next to Lane.

"Don't you take another chance like that! Time's on our side." Lane grabbed Harper by the arm.

"He's changing clips. I just wanted him to know we'd shoot back. If he moves around to one of our flanks, we won't have a chance against that weapon." Harper looked left. "Where's that damned dog?"

Another burst of automatic fire smashed into the rear of the Chev. The air filled with the raw stench of gasoline. Lane and Harper eased their guns out over the hood and fired in Blake's general direction.

Blake stopped firing.

"Can you hear if he's trying to work his way around us?" Harper asked.

"No."

The clicking of the cooling engine sounded unnaturally loud in Lane's ears. They both concentrated, waiting for any sound that might give away Blake's position.

The chainsaw clatter of an approaching helicopter soon made that impossible. They looked up to see the blue-black belly of the helicopter as it came in low and fast. After its first pass, it climbed and hovered over the scene, working its way back and forth over the Chev and the Ford pickup.

The smell of gasoline was stronger now. Lane looked at his knees. A stream of gasoline passed between the detectives and began to fill a hollow at the bottom of the ditch.

"It's times like this I'm glad you don't smoke," Harper said.

"I guess we stay put until we get some help. He hasn't fired at the helicopter, so he must be keeping his head down." Lane lifted his right knee and moved away from the gasoline without leaving the protection of the front of the car.

"Staying put may not be such a good idea if this ignites." Harper peered around the fender.

"Got your cellphone?" Lane asked.

"In the trunk."

"Mine must be on the front seat." Lane thought, *Maybe I should crawl over and get it*.

Harper, as if reading Lane's mind, said, "Stay put."

The helicopter swung south toward the river and made a low pass over them with its nose down. Lane and Harper waved at the pilot and passenger. The helicopter swooped over the house and climbed before returning to hover to the east side of the road.

"What the hell is going on?" Harper asked.

Lane thought, *A joke might lighten the situation up a bit*.

"I wonder if they'll give us another new car?"

Harper smiled. "Two cars in as many weeks. I wonder if it's some kind of record?"

The officer was dressed in black, carried an automatic rifle over one shoulder and his helmet in the other. He marched along the ditch behind them. "Hey guys!"

Lane and Harper turned with their pistols aimed.

The TACTICAL officer held his hands above his head. "I'm one of the good guys."

"Shit," Harper said.

Lane recognized him too. Short hair, a swagger, and an open mouth. It was Stockwell.

Stockwell walked closer. "We've been trying to call you!"

Lane wanted to say, "Sorry, but we were a little preoccupied dodging bullets from an assault rifle."

Harper said, "Ever been shot at?"

"Ummm." Stockwell looked at Lane and grinned.

Lane watched Stockwell's eyes and thought, *You're thinking of a way to sidestep the question. You're so transparent.*

There wasn't a hint of friendliness in Stockwell's smile. "Heard you got wounded last week. Shot in the ass. Was it good for you!?"

Harper moved forward. He cocked his arm, aiming to throw a punch. Lane put a hand on Harper's wrist to hold him back.

Stockwell walked closer. He was near enough to touch them. "Who's the marksman?"

Lane and Harper looked at one another.

They looked back at Stockwell.

"Well, somebody made a hell of a shot." Stockwell wiped his forearm against a sweaty forehead. "Put a bullet in the guy's ear. Dead before he hit the ground. None of us got here in time to take a shot. To make that shot with a Glock is …"

"Impossible," Harper said.

Lane leaned forward. His stomach gave him very little warning. Nauseated by the realization that he might have killed Blake, Lane threw up on Stockwell's boots.

Stockwell danced backwards in horror. "What the fuck?"

"Nice shooting, Lane." Harper rubbed the back of his partner's neck and looked at Stockwell. "Right on target."

Stockwell said, "What's this? Are the two of you sweethearts now?"

Ten minutes later, Harper and Lane sat in the shade and talked on borrowed cellphones. Both of their phones had been chewed up by Blake's gunfire. They watched a fire department crew cleaning up the gasoline in the ditch before the tow truck was allowed to take the Chev away.

"I'm fine. Harper's fine. The only guy hurt was the shooter." Lane waited for Arthur to respond.

"Are you going to make a habit of this?" Arthur asked.

"What? Getting shot at or having our cars wrecked?" Lane took a sip from a bottle of water someone had handed him. *My mouth still tastes like puke,* he thought.

"When will you be home? I want to see you for myself."

"Can't tell you for sure. They'll be done with us eventually. Fire department is here. Forensics is here. It's like a convention." Lane looked around at the collection of vehicles and people. Dr. Fibre walked alongside the Quonset then disappeared behind it.

Lane turned his attention to Deputy Chief Calvin Smoke, who faced the cameras. He wore a goatee and tailor-made dress uniform. Smoke's voice carried over to the detectives. "A suspect has been shot. Two of my detectives are safe. As usual my officers risked their lives to keep my community safe. Good old-fashioned police work, that's my style." Smoke pointed a finger at his chest.

Arthur's voice cracked in Lane's ear. "Matt's at the dance tonight. We have to pick him up at ten."

"You okay?" Lane turned to watch two men pick up Blake's bagged body and place it on a gurney.

"Yep. Bye." Arthur hung up.

Lane looked at Harper, who was on another cell-phone. "It's okay, Erinn. I'm okay. How are you and Jessica?"

Harper looked at Lane. For a moment, they both smiled at this shared experience.

"Glenn's there with you?" Harper asked.

Lane looked at the Quonset. Fibre appeared and beckoned his crew. All were dressed in matching white "bunny suits".

"Good. I'll be home as soon as I can." Harper closed the phone. "She's crying. Jessica's crying, and Glenn's trying to figure out what's going on."

Lane burped and tasted bile. He took another swig of water. He turned to watch the cameras and lights.

"My mandate is to keep the peace and that's just what I intend to do." Deputy Chief Smoke pointed to his left. "Officers like Stockwell here are a fine example of the new, heroic approach to policing." Smoke waved a smiling Stockwell closer.

"Sounds like Smoke wants to be chief," Harper said.

Lane smiled when he saw Smoke's nose wrinkle after he caught the stench of vomit rising from Stockwell's boots. "Seems like Smoke's gotten wind of something unpleasant."

Harper laughed. "That about sums it up. There's a joke that some cops pass around. They call it being "Smoked". It's another word for getting screwed. If you put a pin up against Smoke's ego, you end up on a shit detail like dealing with drunks at a football game."

Lane looked toward the curved wall of the Quonset.

"What are you thinking?" Harper asked.

"I don't know how we hit Blake," Lane said.

"I can't figure it out either. He had to be facing us. I only took five shots and there are five hits in the truck. That's what I was aiming at." He looked at the black Ford pickup. Its front license plate read "Republic of Alberta".

"My magazine is missing four rounds. I was sure I fired over his head." Lane searched his memory for a logical answer.

"Guess we have to wait for the autopsy." Harper looked at the Quonset. Fibre had a shovel in his hands. "Wonder what they found over there?"

Lane looked around at the various people working the scene then at Smoke smiling at the reporters. "They've forgotten about us. Let's go and see what Fibre's up to." He started across the gravel driveway, heals scuffing against the uneven surface, before turning onto the grass.

Harper walked beside him. At the barbed-wire fence, he held the top wire with his hand and the bottom two with his foot. Lane ducked through the gap, turned and held the wire for Harper.

They heard the sound of shovels shifting earth and grinding against stone. They rounded the end of the shed. Fibre was on his elbows and knees. With the hood of his white suit covering his head, he could have passed for a rabbit on steroids. The stink of decomposition mixed with freshly turned earth made Lane cover his nose. He thought, *This is going to make me sick again.*

Two of Fibre's assistants lifted a plastic bag from the shallow grave. A dog's paw poked out of hole in the green plastic.

Harper held his hand over his face. "Rosco?"

"We need a tarp to lay the bag on!" Fibre looked at Lane. "What are *you* doing here?" Fibre hesitated for a moment. "There's a tarp in the unit. Get it!" One of the assistants laughed at Lane's discomfort.

Lane took his time walking back to the forensics vehicle while thinking, *Fibre has a great mind when it comes to dealing with the dead but absolutely no idea when it comes to dealing with the living.*

"I'm not going in there!" Christine sat down on the grass in front of the Jeep. Roz was tied to Christine by her leash, and as a result, to the drama. The dog looked pleadingly over her shoulder at Lane and Harper while they walked toward the church.

The sun was setting. Shades of purples, oranges, and pinks painted the sky. Lane leaned back and took it in. *It feels good to see this,* he thought. He looked at the grey, blue stuccoed building with an attached gymnasium.

Arthur looked at his watch. "We'd better get this over with." He looked around the parking lot, expecting someone to jump out and point a finger at them. Every second vehicle was a minivan or something more substantial. It was an aquarium of vehicles with fish on their bumpers. Fish on their hatches. Truth fish eating Darwin fish. "I was just thinking. Do you want to try some fish this week? How about some rainbow trout?"

There was no time for us to talk, Lane thought, *that's why Arthur's acting like this. It's just that with these kids there's never any time for anything but handling the next crisis.*

Arthur hurried ahead. "Hurry up! This place gives me the creeps. Any second two guys with white shirts, ties, and name tags will try to convert us."

Lane looked back at Christine. She glared at them while rubbing the dog under the chin. Roz smiled, revealing her canines.

"Come on." Arthur led the way to the front entrance.

Lane thought he recognized the beat of The Village People pounding through the walls. *Impossible*, he thought.

They walked through the front doors. An unattended table was set up in the hallway. "Adam & Eve: The Dance" was the sign taped to the front of the table. Behind it, on the wall, were black T-shirts on sale with "*God said Adam & Eve* NOT *Adam and Steve*" stencilled on them in white letters.

Arthur's ears turned red. "Hurry up." He threw the comment over his shoulder and plowed forward into the music. They turned a corner.

"YMCA!"

They stepped into a gymnasium or meeting hall, it was hard to tell which.

Lights flashed along the stage. A group of teens danced in a line along the edge. They made a Y with their arms and bodies.

The kids on the floor shouted, "M! C! A!"

The arms raised in the crowd, and the arms raised

along the stage, made human approximations of the letters.

Lane felt the pounding of bass against his ribcage.

"Where is he?" Arthur looked over the crowd.

The music died down as the song ended. The kids looked at one another.

"Can you believe this?" Lane scanned the crowd looking for Matt.

"What? Believe what?" Arthur looked behind Lane.

"The music, I mean doesn't anyone here know that The Village People are ..."

"IN THE NAVY!" The volume of the next song sent a shock wave running through the crowd.

Lane smiled.

"He's not here!" Arthur's eyes got even wider.

"Let's check outside!"

"What?" Arthur cupped his left hand over the back of his ear.

Lane took him by the arm and went out a back door. The door shut behind them. Lane and Arthur stood stunned by the silence and the rainbow of colours in the sky. Their Jeep was parked thirty metres away.

In front of the Jeep, Matt and Christine sat on the grass on either side of the dog. Matt's shoulders sagged. Christine put her arm around him. Roz licked his face.

Lane caught Arthur by the arm. "Give them a minute."

Arthur looked at Lane. "I don't get it. All they do is fight."

After a minute they walked toward Matt, Roz, and Christine who were climbing into the Jeep.

Arthur got into the driver's seat. Lane walked around to the other side.

Arthur started the engine as Lane climbed in.

"Uncle Lane, Matt's got something to say to you," Christine said.

Lane locked his seat belt, winced at the sore muscles of his chest and backside, and turned to face Matt.

Arthur reversed.

"How come you never asked me about the marionettes?" Matt asked.

Where did this come from? Lane saw the tears in Matt's eyes. "Marionettes?"

Arthur stopped, shifted into drive, and headed out of the parking lot.

Matt nodded. "Harper asked Glenn if he knew anything about marionettes, because it has something to do with the case you're working on."

Lane heard the accusation in Matt's voice.

Lane said, "Yes it does."

"I know all about marionettes. We're studying about them in drama. Didn't you know that?" Matt turned to Christine for support.

Lane's mind raced. *How did I get into the middle of this mess? It's one car wreck after another.* "What do you know?"

"During the Second World War the Czechs used marionettes to satirize Hitler, among other things." Matt looked directly at his uncle. "The artist would let the marionette say things that were against the government and controversial while making the audience laugh."

Lane's mind bounced back and forth between what he'd just learned and the feeling that he was under attack. "I didn't know."

"Or didn't care," Matt said.

"What?" *What did I do?* Lane thought.

"You've been so busy with the case and so busy with Christine, you've hardly talked with me. It hurts." Matt turned to look out the window.

Lane thought, *I'm always one or two steps behind these two, just like I'm one or two steps behind this case.*

"I'm exhausted!" Alex put the back of his marionette hand to his forehead and acted as if he were about to faint.

"Drama queen." Aidan leaned against the wall, unimpressed.

"Drag king." Alex sighed. "How many times do we have to go over this?"

Aidan looked thoughtful. "Until we leave no doubt in their minds that we're real, that this is real, and what happened to you was real. That's when we'll be ready."

"Of course we're real. Just because I'm dead doesn't mean I'm a ghost!"

"That's what the audience needs to understand. As long as we're here, on this stage, we have to be real in their minds. Then they'll understand." Aidan leaned away from the wall.

"Understand what?"

"If you don't know, how the hell will they?" Aidan's voice was so jammed full of emotion that Alex stumbled back as if struck by the force of it.

"Quit playing the drama queen and get on with your story!" Aidan put her fists on her hips. "You say all of this," in one graceful sweep, her hand travelled from left to right, "will help me deal with what happened. So, put your considerable dramatic talent to good use and prove it!"

TUESDAY, JULY 9

ch*a*pter 12

Kuldeep put coffee and sandwiches in front of Lane and Harper. Lane looked out the window and thought, *It looks and smells like rain.* The sky was a dark purple-grey.

"So, what have we got? I mean do we start from square one, close the case or pick up somewhere in the middle?" Harper lifted his sandwich and took a bite.

"Once we get Fibre's autopsy report, then we'll have a better idea. I still think we've got another shooter. There's no way I made that shot." Lane took a sip of coffee and felt the warmth travelling into his belly. He took another drink.

Harper spoke from behind his hand. "You're forgetting the ricochet that hit you. If it could happen once to you at Eva's, it could happen again to Blake."

"That's not it. A nine millimetre bullet would make a bigger entrance wound and there would probably be an exit wound in Blake's skull. In all probability, the bullet that hit Blake was of a smaller calibre."

Harper smiled. "You're starting to sound all analytical like me."

Lane laughed. "You still going to the rodeo?"

"I've been told by Erinn and Glenn that I have to be there. What's it like? I mean, I've never been." Harper looked out the window. The first wind-driven rain was sliding down the glass.

"It's ... I don't know. You have to be there. It's outrageous, fun, irreverent, real." Lane lifted his hands away from the coffee cup and shrugged.

"Kind of like Arthur?"

"Kind of." Lane thought about Arthur, how he'd been coping alone with two teens, and whether or not their relationship would survive the experience. *And how will I make things right with Matt?* "When does Fibre think the initial findings of the medical examiner will be ready?"

"Today."

Lane said, "And I have to see my doctor today."

Three hours later, Lane visited Dr. Keeler's office. Lane's doctor was an invaluable source for almost all things medical. In the past, his keen mind had revealed pivotal information to Lane. Harper waited a block away in a coffee shop on Fourth Avenue.

Dr. Keeler's nurse, Mavis, fussed over Lane as soon as she spotted him in the waiting room. She picked up his chart, looked over top of the manila folder and glared. "Lane. You're next."

Lane felt as inconsequential as he always did when he stood next to her. She towered over him, wore nothing but white, outweighed him by fifty pounds, and could clean up the floor with him if the notion ever took hold of her. "Good to see you again, Mavis." He followed her down the hallway lined with examination rooms. She opened the last door on the right and let him in first, then she stood in the doorway.

"You didn't follow his advice to take some time off work, did you?" Mavis could sound like the voice of doom. Today was getting pretty close to Armageddon.

"We're in the middle of a homicide investigation." Lane thought, *It sounds like I'm whining.*

Mavis put her hands on her hips and glared. "Just be glad *I'm* not taking those stitches out! You need to take better care of yourself! Was that you who was shot at yesterday?"

Lane went to answer and decided against it.

"So it was you!" Mavis pointed her finger at him.

"Yes." Lane looked at the carpet. It was industrial blue grey.

"What happens to Arthur and Matt if you don't come home? They've both been through enough this last year!"

"Don't forget Christine," Lane said without thinking. *Oh no! Now Mavis will really let me have it!* he thought.

"Christine? Who's she?" Mavis' eyes targeted Lane.

"My niece. She just arrived."

"How did you end up with two kids?" Mavis' tone softened.

"She just arrived on our doorstep like Matt did." Lane looked at Mavis' green eyes, knew he had touched her soft spot, and realized he was not above taking advantage.

"You took her in, just like that?" She crossed her arms.

"Christine had no place else to go. They excommunicated her."

"Who's they?" Mavis' voice rose again.

"The guys running Paradise." Lane sat down in the chair and began unlacing his shoes.

"You mean that polygamist community south of here?" Mavis looked sideways at him.

"That's the one." Lane took his socks off.

"Sounds like your niece was lucky to get thrown out."

Lane looked up at Mavis. "I hope so."

"And now you've got two kids who need you at home. So, take better care of yourself!" Mavis slammed the door behind her.

And I thought talking about Christine was calming her down. Lane stripped down to his underwear and stood next to the examination table.

Dr. Keeler walked in. After closing the door, he looked at the chart and then at Lane. "How are you?" Keeler held out his hand.

Lane shook it. "Better."

"What was Mavis upset about?" Keeler studied Lane's reactions.

He's getting grey, Lane thought. *And he's put on a bit of weight.* "She was just looking out for me."

"You mean you're back at work?" Keeler crossed his arms across the chart held against his chest.

"That's right." Lane waited for the second eruption.

"This is related to the deaths of the four guys who lived west of town?" Keeler put the chart down next to the sink and sat in the chair.

"Actually it may have been five." Lane reached around with his right hand and scratched his left shoulder.

"Really? Would you get on your belly, and I'll take a look at how your wound is healing."

Lane eased onto his stomach. The cold from the black vinyl beneath the paper sheet gave him goose bumps. "On the first and second anniversaries of a seventeen-year-old's death, two young men disappeared."

Keeler eased Lane's underwear down. "No infection. the bruising is vivid. There's a rainbow of yellows, purples, and greens here. So, you think the first death, that of the seventeen-year-old, is related to the disappearances?"

"It's a distinct possibility." Lane gritted his teeth as Keeler used his fingers to prod a tender spot next to the wound.

"I've been following the case and I was wondering." Keeler moved to the sink and washed his hands. "There might be two killers."

Lane looked at Keeler. "How do you come to that conclusion?"

"One's very discreet and patient. The victims disappear on a specific date and are yet to be found. The other is especially violent. A body is found very quickly, if not immediately. The murders don't appear to follow the same pattern."

Lane thought, *It's possible.*

"Mavis will be right in." Keeler made for the door.

"Why Mavis?" Lane raised up on his elbows.

"Next time, do as we tell you. Take some time off." Keeler shut the door.

A minute later, Mavis opened the door. She carried a tray covered with a cloth. She pulled two surgical gloves from a package. "I'm back."

Harper was waiting with a cup of coffee when Lane returned to the waiting room.

In the elevator, Harper said, "You look a little worse for wear."

"Actually, it wasn't all bad." His phone rang. He reached into his pocket and flipped open his cell. "Lane."

The voice was toneless, "Dr. Colin Weaver here."

Lane looked at Harper and mouthed, "Fibre." Lane kept his tone even. "Do you have some information to share?"

"Yes." Weaver's tone seldom varied from monotone.

Lane waited. The silence stretched out like summer honey. "Well?"

"There were several significant findings." Weaver took a long breath.

"Could I have them in order, please?" Lane rolled his eyes. Harper smiled.

"Most significant to least?" Fibre asked.

"Certainly."

Fibre continued without taking a breath. "Mr. Blake Rogers died from a single gunshot wound. The bullet entered the left ear canal. Death was instantaneous. The bullet was .22 calibre. It has still to be inspected by a ballistics expert but initial findings, and I'm quite confident here, are that the bullet matches the one taken from the scene where you were wounded." Fibre took a breath. "Also, the bullets from the rifle in Mr. Blake

Rogers' possession fired bullets of the same calibre found several days ago at his house. Again the match has to be verified by ballistics, and again I'm confident they are, in fact, identical." Fibre took another breath. "The indentation in the dog's skull matches the bat found with the body. The indentation found in Skip Lombardi's skull was also similar. Blood and tissue was found on the bat. We are now attempting to find DNA matches for these samples. Results will be made available to you as soon as they become available to us."

"So you're saying that the bat used to kill the dog may be the same weapon used to kill Lombardi?" Lane asked.

"As of yet, I cannot confirm that finding. It is, however, a distinct possibility."

"Thank you. I appreciate your call." Lane waited for Fibre to hang up.

"So, what did Fibre have to say?" Harper handed Lane the cup of coffee as they exited the elevator.

"The same thing my doctor said, actually." Lane took a sip and closed his eyes, feeling the warmth of the coffee on the inside and, as they stepped out the door, the sun on the outside.

"It looks like we've got more than one killer. Fibre's almost certain that the bullet they took out of me is a match for the one that killed Blake." Lane looked across the street at the two-storey homes lined up cheek to cheek. He took another sip of coffee and tasted the chocolate. "And they're checking out the bat that was buried with Rosco."

"DNA?" Harper walked to the Chev and opened the driver's door.

"Yes. It'll take a day or two." Lane opened the passenger door. That new car smell reached his nostrils. "Should we take a drive out west and see if we can get another new car tomorrow?" Lane regretted the joke when he saw Harper shudder from a flashback.

Alex the marionette sat in a chair across from Aidan. Up top, above the marionettes, Aidan wore a royal blue silk western-cut shirt and a pair of black jodhpurs. Her tan riding boots reached just below the knee. She wore a black ball cap. Aidan's marionette was dressed exactly the same.

Alex said, "The problem is with what happens to you after the show. More than a few people aren't gonna be happy with what you have to say. And we both know what can happen when you take a stand. Eva took a stand. Look what happened to me!"

Aidan put her hand on his shoulder. She pushed back her ball cap and used her worst cowboy accent to say, "Y'all know a drag king does what a drag king's got to do."

Alex raised his head and smiled. "So, you want me to saddle up, do ya?"

"That's right."

"Remember what happened the last time I rode a horse? It took the high side of the ditch and brushed up against a tree. When I leaned away, the saddle slipped and I ended up at the bottom of the ditch with my face up against a beer can."

"You survived," Aidan said.

"Yes, that time I did. And that's my point. I died in a ditch. I don't want the same thing happening to you."

"Blake's dead," Aidan said.

Alex laughed. "You just don't get it. There's always another Blake around. All you have to do is wait at the side of the highway, and he or she'll be along before too long."

"If I don't do this, it will be like I backed away from what happened to you. Like I let you and Eva down." Aidan looked off-stage.

"Just don't get yourself killed over it. My grandmother's not as strong as she looks."

Lane noted there was a lull in traffic at the gas station. Harper reversed into a parking stall and they got out. Through the glass they could see the young woman with black hair watching them from the other side.

"Think she remembers us?" Harper opened the door for Lane.

Inside, they heard the hum of fridges and air conditioning. Lane saw that Kelsey wore a short-sleeved shirt. He wondered how she handled the cold. On the wall was the poster of a cowboy posing with a rifle. The caption: *Keep your city out of my country.*

"Do you have a couple of minutes for a question or two?" Harper asked.

Kelsey turned white. "Has someone else been shot? People around here are still pretty upset."

"No. We just wanted to clarify what happened the day of the shooting at Blake Rogers' acreage." Harper stepped no closer to her.

"Okay." Kelsey sat on a stool behind the counter. She crossed her arms under her breasts.

"Who arrived first?" Lane asked.

"Eva. She and Norm drove up in her pickup. They were on their way back from getting groceries. The truck's box was filled with bags of food. Norm doesn't drive. Can't. Eva takes him into town when he needs food or clothes. She's been taking care of him since Norm's mom died. Norm got out of the truck to fill it with gas."

"Eva takes care of Norm?" Harper leaned against the window of a cooler filled with soft drinks.

"For the last few years she has. Norm's kind of slow. Somethin' happened to him when he was a kid. Eva and Norm's mom were friends. The story is that Eva promised to look out for him when Norm's mom got sick. That's why he helps her with sweat lodges."

"Does he live with her?" Harper asked.

"Nope. He has a little place of his own. Far as I know, only Aidan lives with Eva now." Kelsey glanced to her left as a truck pulled up to the pumps.

"Aidan?" Lane watched Kelsey as she leaned over and activated the pump.

"Yep. Aidan and Alex were friends. Aidan was there when he was killed. Aidan's lived with Eva ever since her parents moved to Australia or something. Haven't seen Aidan around for a week or two. Every anniversary is hard on her. She got arrested one year. Rumour is she's cookin' up something special for this anniversary." Kelsey watched the driver fill up his truck.

"Like what?" Lane watched Kelsey's eyes.

"Some kind of theatre or something. She was workin' on it all winter but not talkin' about it much. She used to fill up on her way in or out of town. She was always haulin' paint or wood or fabric. Stuff like that.

Whenever I asked what she was up to, she'd say, 'Come and see the show'."

"Is there anything else you remember?" Harper asked.

"Everybody figured it was Blake who ran Alex down. There was bad blood between Blake's family and Eva. He was always shootin' his mouth off about how he wished Alberta would become a republic so there'd be no more land claims. He said Eva was just a freeloader who didn't work and got paid for stayin' at home. I used to laugh when he said that. Nobody around here could ever remember *Blake* havin' a job. Instead, he was always tryin' to act macho. Everybody knew he was a real head case. The problem was, after Alex died, nobody could prove Blake had somethin' to do with the killing, and no one who lived with Blake was talkin'." Kelsey looked out the window. The driver of the pickup finished filling one tank and started on the next.

Lane looked at Harper.

"It's startin' to get busy here." Kelsey nodded out the window.

A motor home and a minivan pulled up to the pumps.

"We're done for now. Thanks," Harper said.

"Do you know where Norm lives?" Lane asked.

"Close to Eva's." Kelsey activated two more pumps.

"Thanks." Lane held the door open for Harper.

Once inside the car, Lane said, "Refresh my memory about Aidan."

"I met her when you were in the sweat lodge. Norm and I helped load up the stuff for her show." Harper turned the key.

"Stuff?" Lane put on his seatbelt.

Harper shifted into drive and pulled out. "She has marionettes and some kind of set she's built. It's really beautiful woodwork. She's got talent. And, she's got an attitude."

"There's a lot of that going around." Lane thought, *Sounds just like Christine and Matt.*

"Trouble at home?" Harper asked.

"Matt says I haven't been paying enough attention to him."

"That's good news." Harper smiled.

"How's that?" Lane asked.

"He wants you to spend more time with him instead of not wanting you around at all."

It took fifteen minutes to drive to Eva's place. For the last three minutes, they were guided by a column of white smoke rising to about three hundred metres into a cloudless sky where the smoke was flattened by an upper-level wind out of the west.

Harper cautiously entered Eva's yard. Eva and Norm sat in lawn chairs drinking coffee and watching the fire, which was situated about ten metres south of the sweat lodge.

Harper circled the yard and pointed the nose of the Chev toward the lane leading out of the yard and back to the main road.

They got out of the car. Lane looked at Eva, who smiled and lifted a pot of coffee as an invitation.

"Where did Norm disappear to?" Harper asked.

Norm reappeared from the shadows of the Quonset with a pair of lawn chairs. He handed one to Harper. Norm walked over to Lane. "This one's for you. It's the softest one we got." He opened it and handed it to Lane. "You here to arrest Eva?"

"No. And thanks for the chair." Lane wondered about the unexpected kindness and Norm's question.

"Good. We're just watchin' the fire burn down." Norm sat down in the chair next to Eva. He wasn't wearing a cap. A scar ran along the crown of his forehead. There was a ridge, like an elongated speed bump, beneath the scar.

Lane looked at Norm's empty gun holster. "Where did you get that?"

"Mom gave it to me for Christmas. Long time ago." Norm stared into the fire.

"Pour yourself a cup." Eva pointed at the end table crowded with two cups, a pot of coffee, a container of milk, and some sugar cubes on a plate.

Norm got up, poured a cup and handed it to Lane.

"Thanks." Lane eased back into the chair.

"Looks like you were expecting us." Harper poured himself a cup and sat down.

"Healin' up okay?" Norm looked at Lane.

"Better every day." Lane took a sip of coffee and wondered at how much better it seemed to taste out here.

Eva watched Lane and Harper with friendly curiousity. "Figure you two must be a little gun-shy. Seems like you come out here to get shot at."

Lane laughed. "It's just like being at home."

Eva looked at him for a moment. "Kids in trouble?"

"They're fighting with each other. Then they're mad at me." Lane watched as a timber burned through. A rock tumbled down into the mound of embers at the bottom of the fire pit.

Eva shrugged. "That's kids. When I came back from residential school, I was lost. After that, it took a little while to find myself. Maybe your two are finding themselves."

Norm stayed quiet, apparently contemplating the fire.

Lane thought, *Is that what Matt and Christine are doing? Finding themselves?*

"How's Aidan doing?" Harper asked.

"Called last night. Sounded tired. Her show's nearly ready for the rodeo." Eva sat up and leaned a bit closer to the fire.

"Stampede?" Lane asked.

"It's her first show and she's nervous." Norm sounded like he was hypnotized by the fire.

"She lives here?" Lane found he was staring into the orange heart of the fire.

"Since before Alex died. She'll fight the land claim after I'm gone. And maybe my daughter will come back some day and the land will be here for her too." Eva wrapped her fingers around the cup.

Harper balanced his coffee on the arm of his chair. "Who's the best shot around here?"

Eva looked at each of the detectives in turn. "Enough questions. Time for some quiet. There's no reason for anybody to do any more shootin'."

"Watch the news this morning? Line-ups of people at the grocery stores wanting to buy bottled water. City people always actin' crazy." Norm shook his head. "Then there's the gangs. You guys ever have to deal with gangs? People out here worry about the trouble the city will bring with it."

Lane and Harper looked at one another. Lane smiled. *Eva and Norm sure know how to get a conversation side-tracked when they want to.*

Harper said, "I've met a few gang members."

Norm leaned forward. His lawn chair complained. "What're they like?"

"Loners. Kids mostly. Young people looking for a place to belong. Trying to find themselves, just like Eva says." Harper looked at the fire.

Eva said, "Sounds like they're pretty much like the rest of us."

"You're coming for a walk with us, Uncle Lane." There was a challenge in Christine's eyes as she watched him from across the kitchen table.

He looked at the aftermath of Arthur's barbecued chicken. The platter was empty, just like the salad bowl and bread basket. Matt's eyes were glazed with satisfaction, and he half smiled.

Arthur snored on the couch.

Christine covered her ears. She turned to Lane. "How do you get any sleep?"

Lane shrugged. He stood, groaned when his back muscles complained and began gathering the dishes, carrying them to the counter and opening the dishwasher.

Matt stirred from his stupor to carry the platter and bowl.

Christine grabbed the washcloth to wipe the table and counter.

As they finished, Lane thought, *We made short work of that.*

"Come on. Roz needs a walk." Christine walked to the back door.

At the sound of the word "walk", the dog raised her head.

When Christine and Lane grabbed plastic bags to stuff in their pockets, Roz was on her feet. Her tongue hung out the side of her mouth. Her ears were up and facing forward. She began to jump at the front door.

"Come on, Matt." Christine grabbed Roz's collar and hooked the leash on.

Matt bent to put on his shoes. Roz circled him, wrapping the leash around his legs. "Roz!" Matt turned in the opposite direction, picked up the leash, then stepped out the door. Roz ran and hit the end of the leash, nearly turning Matt's elbow inside out. "Roz! Slow down!" She dragged him down the steps and along the sidewalk. Lane and Christine followed behind the wheezing dog and complaining Matt.

"Wait for us!" Christine ran to keep up with Matt, who always appeared to be on the verge of tripping and falling.

Matt lurched along behind Roz, who was pulling a sled to the North Pole, or at least as far as the off-leash area. "You take her then!"

It took ten minutes to get to the opening in the chain link fence. Matt was thirty metres ahead. The evening sun was casting shadows. Lane watched Matt step inside the off-leash area and lean down.

"Wait!" Lane said.

Matt released the dog, looked back at Lane and shrugged.

"Don't worry," Christine patted her uncle's shoulder, "she never lets you out of her sight. Just like Matt and me."

Lane looked at her. "What do you mean?"

"We like to keep you around. Know where you are. We're strays, just like Roz." Christine squeezed his shoulder.

To Lane, the touch of her hand felt like a benediction. He went to answer her and found he could not.

In the evening light, Roz's tail revealed the gold under the black when she ran to the top of the hill. She disappeared over the crest.

Lane and Christine caught up to Matt, who was bent double in an effort to catch his breath. He stood up and looked at Christine. "Did you tell him?"

"I will when I'm ready!" Christine marched ahead, her spine suddenly stiff with anger.

Above her, Roz poked her head over the crest of the hill, saw that they were following and disappeared.

"What are you talking about?" Lane asked.

"Christine wanted to talk to you about stuff." Matt walked a metre or two behind Lane as they walked up the gravel pathway. On either side there was tough, blue-grey prairie grass. Lane reached the top of the first hill.

"Stuff?" Lane thought, *How come it's so easy to get into all kinds of trouble?*

"You know. Paradise. You getting shot at. Arthur. All that stuff." Matt reached the top where a valley and larger hill greeted them. Ahead, Christine ran up the second hill while Roz sniffed at a bush before running up to another.

A jackrabbit hopped out of the brush ahead of the dog. The grey-tan rabbit stopped and stood on its hind legs. Roz looked at the rabbit and barked once. The rabbit launched itself up the next hill.

Dust puffed up behind Roz as she gave chase. Christine screamed something unintelligible and ran faster.

"Roz!" Lane ran after the dog thinking of the hole in the fence below the hill where a construction crew worked along the edge of four lanes of freeway.

Christine disappeared over the top of the second hill.

Lane reached the crest about thirty seconds later with Matt about three strides behind.

They stopped and looked down. The angle was almost too steep to travel down. A zigzag trail traversed the eastern slope. Christine was sliding straight down on her backside, trailing a cloud of dust. Below, a yellow backhoe scooped earth from a hole and dumped it into the back of a dump truck.

Roz tried to cut inside of the arc of the turning jackrabbit. It zipped between the backhoe and truck. Roz lost her footing and tumbled. The backhoe emptied its bucket into the back of the truck. Lane heard Christine's scream snuffed by the *whump* of soil and rock hitting the truck's metal box.

A cloud of dust rose up and swirled around the truck. Christine was on her feet and running. Lane watched her disappear into the cloud.

It took time for Lane and Matt to make their way

to the bottom. The operator had stopped the backhoe. The driver was out of his truck. Lane and Matt rounded the front of the truck. Sound was smothered by the idling diesels.

The truck driver was on his hands and knees at the edge of the hole. He reached down. His hand disappeared. He lifted Roz out of the hole by her collar. When he set her down, she shook the dust off her coat.

The driver reached down a second time. He pulled Christine out of the hole. She sat on the lip with her back facing them. Abruptly, she swung her legs around to get both feet underneath her.

As she leaned forward, the dog came over and licked her face. Christine wiped her face with the back of her hand. A smear of mud reached from her right eye to her ear.

The truck driver was the first to laugh.

Matt was the second.

Lane couldn't decide if he was laughing from relief or something else altogether.

After a few minutes, they followed the dog along a gentler slope that would eventually lead them back to where they started.

Even Roz stopped at the top. Her tongue hung out and she lay down with her belly against the cool grass. Matt rubbed her neck.

Lane looked back. The downtown towers stood above the expanse of urban forest.

"Did you ever meet my dad?" Christine asked.

"Twice." Lane turned to study her eyes. Out of the corner of his eye he could see Matt watching them.

"Will you tell me the truth?" Christine blinked.

"Yes." Lane watched her eyes filling with tears.

"What was he like?"

"He was married and his wife was expecting a child. Your mother got in touch with him when she found out she was pregnant with you, but it didn't go well."

"Well?" Christine wiped at her eyes, creating more muddy smudges.

"He was a football player."

"And?"

Lane took a breath. "When your mother talked to him, he denied that he was the father."

"Oh." Christine looked over the city. Roz got up and put her head in Christine's lap. "Are you going to be around much longer?"

Lane looked at Matt and then back at Christine. "I'm here. I don't plan on going anywhere."

"But you got shot," Matt said.

"And Arthur cries when you go to work." Christine looked up at her uncle.

Lane opened his mouth to reply and closed it. *How do I answer this one?* "Are you two coming to the rodeo with us?"

"Are you going to be there?" Christine and Matt asked at the same time.

"Yes." Lane looked at each of them in turn.

"What the hell happened to you?" Arthur stood at the back door. Christine sat in a lawn chair to empty dirt from her shoes.

"She fell in a hole," Matt said.

Christine glared at Matt.

"You what?" Arthur stood next to Christine and picked a piece of dirt from her hair.

"I was looking for Roz, and I fell in." Christine looked up at Arthur.

He saw the streak of mud along her cheek. Arthur looked at the dog. "You both need a bath."

Roz howled when Christine took the dog into the shower. Matt waited outside the downstairs bathroom door with towels to catch and dry a reluctant Roz.

The soothing scent of chicken, ginger, sesame oil, and lemon still filled the kitchen where Lane and Arthur waited.

Arthur poured boiling water into the tea pot.

"The kids told me you're worried." Lane set the fourth tea cup down.

"We've had a hell of a year. My sister died. And everything else that's happened. Of course I'm worried." Arthur set the tea pot on a ceramic hot plate in the center of the table. The scent of mint mixed with the others.

"Can we go to the rodeo?" Lane smiled.

"You'd better be there." Arthur unplugged the kettle.

The door of the bathroom opened. There was the sound of Roz's nails slipping on hardwood.

"Roz!" Matt said.

The dog ran up to the top of the stairs, entered the kitchen, looked at Lane and Arthur, then shook the water off her back. It splattered the front of the fridge and Lane as he bent to grab Roz.

Arthur opened the door to the deck. Roz scooted outside.

Lane grabbed a tea towel and wiped his face. Then he used it to wipe the fridge and the floor.

"You'd better be there," Arthur said.

Lane looked at his partner. "Count on it."

"What did you call me?!" Matt's voice was accented with outrage.

"A cripple!" Christine said.

"Don't you ever call me that again!" Matt said.

"Then stop callin' me a bitch!" Christine said.

Arthur and Lane looked at one another as if to say, "Here we go again."

Lane moved to the top of the stairs.

"Keep your clothes on. We're saving that for the next major emergency," Arthur said.

Lane turned.

Arthur offered a wan smile.

WEDNESDAY, JULY 10

ch*a*pter 13

"Fibre wants to see us." Harper drove along Parkdale Boulevard. Joggers and cyclists raced along the pathway between the boulevard and the river. Lane saw two cyclists exchange insults as they passed one another. One ran off the path, hit a low spot in the grass, and went over his handlebars. The other looked over his shoulder, laughing, and promptly disappeared into an evergreen tree.

"There's something you don't see every day," Lane said.

"What?" Harper turned right and up the hill to the hospital.

Lane thought about the way Fibre liked to keep his office cool all year round. "I should have brought warmer clothing."

They found Dr. Colin "Fibre" Weaver waiting for them, wearing a grey tweed jacket, white shirt, and khaki tie. Fibre was pouring over a file in a room with two computers. The room shone with cool air, sparkling metal furniture, spotless glass, and a single filing cabinet. The only paper on the desk was in a manila folder.

Fibre looked up, checked his watch, and did not shake hands. "There have been some unusual findings."

Harper closed the door and sat next to Lane.

"Go ahead." Lane felt the cold vinyl against his back and legs.

"First off." Fibre closed the folder. "The bullets are a match. Ballistics confirms this. The bullet that wounded you, Detective Lane, was fired from the same weapon that killed Blake Rogers. Both are .22 calibre." Fibre spoke in a monotone and looked at an invisible point between Harper and Lane.

Harper shrugged as if to say, "Tell us something new."

"The bullets from Mr. Rogers' weapon are a match with the ones we found in the exterior walls and roof of his house. Also, the angles and patterns of penetration in your damaged vehicle follow the pattern on Mr. Rogers' house. The first shots were near target and subsequent rounds went high. Which, as it turns out, was quite fortunate for the two of you, since his weapon fired large rounds with far greater velocity." Fibre took a breath.

"So you're saying that Blake was a poor shot, and the person who killed him was not," Harper said.

"Person or persons. I try not to make any assumptions whatsoever." Fibre made momentary eye contact with Harper.

Harper made no attempt to hide his frustration. "None of this is news to us."

Fibre smiled.

Lane and Harper looked at one another. If Fibre had stood on his desk and danced, they would have been less shocked.

"At the same time, some fascinating evidence was gathered at the scene where the remains of the deceased dog were unearthed at Blake Rogers' acreage." Fibre turned in his chair.

Lane and Harper leaned forward.

Fibre looked out the window.

Lane thought, *This could go on all day.* "I'm sure Detective Harper meant no offense by his remark."

Fibre turned back.

"I apologize," Harper said.

Fibre's face remained blank. "Human and canine blood were removed from the baseball bat. The human blood type matched Mr. Lombardi. The human hair found on the bat was also consistent with Mr. Lombardi's hair. We are presently awaiting DNA results. It appears the bat I found was the murder weapon." Fibre leaned back in his chair. His arms windmilled as he leaned back a bit too far. For a moment, Fibre was on the edge of going backwards over the chair.

He leaned forward, placed his elbows on the desk, and checked to see if Lane or Harper had noticed the near disaster.

"That *is* new." Harper kept a straight face.

"Anything else?" Lane asked.

"Fingerprints matching those of Mr. Blake Rogers were found on the wooden handle." Fibre adopted a pose which could only be called self-satisfied.

"That is news. Were there any other findings?" Lane asked as he stood.

"Our team continues to examine evidence from the house. We'll keep you informed." Fibre turned and looked out the window.

"Very impressive work, Colin," Lane said.

"Of course." Fibre waved his hand without turning around.

Lane and Harper walked out. In the elevator, Harper raised his eyebrows.

Lane shook his head. *We need to wait until we're in the car,* he thought.

It took five minutes to get back to the car.

"Okay." Harper put the key in the ignition. "What?"

"Fibre's just wacky enough to bug the elevator, that's all." Lane put on his seatbelt.

"So what if he does?" Harper turned on the engine and slipped the transmission into drive.

"He's a valuable source of information. I don't want to offend him."

"You're afraid I'm gonna open my mouth and piss him off?" Harper braked for traffic. He turned down the hill and headed for the river valley.

"Yes." Lane looked across the river at the trees on the bluff.

"Do you want to know more about the land claim?" Harper guided the car around a descending curve in the road.

"There's a coffee shop right around the corner."

"Why did I know you were gonna say that?" Harper smiled.

After ordering coffee, they found a seat at one end of the café, close to a window.

"So, what did you find out?" Lane asked.

"It's more complicated than I thought. You see, the land Blake Rogers lived on has been in his family for nearly one hundred years. One of his ancestors was the minister who worked on the Sarcee Reserve—that's what it was called before T'suu T'ina Nation—and he was deeded the land."

"Here you are." The waiter slid their coffees onto the table.

"Thanks," Lane said.

Harper took a careful sip, smiled and took another. "You've done it again! This is great coffee. How do you find these places?"

"You were saying?" Lane took a sip of his mochachino and wore a mustache of whipped cream.

Harper handed Lane a napkin.

Lane wiped at his lip.

"Forty years ago, Eva bought some of the land back. More recently, she made a claim. She says that the land Blake lived on was originally given to her tribe by treaty. I checked into it. She has a strong case. Blake couldn't sell the land. This is where it gets especially interesting."

Lane waited.

Harper took another sip of coffee. "Blake Rogers was broke. Because his land is now within city limits, it's worth a fortune. Blake wanted to sell part of it but couldn't. He actually owned more than twenty hectares of land. Some of it was rented out. He looked into subdividing some of it but found he could not. In fact, he may have been about to declare bankruptcy."

"Eva tied the land up and messed him up." Lane smiled.

"Apparently, and it looks like Eva will eventually win."

"Are we looking at a motive then?" Lane asked.

"For Alex's murder, but not for the others." Harper looked out the window. A couple in their twenties sat on the terrace soaking up the sun.

"We have five deaths, the four who were residents at Blake's house as well as Alex. Blake had a motive for killing Alex, and we have at least one witness who says that's what he did. The evidence suggests that the same weapon that wounded me, killed Blake. Finally, the evidence points at Blake for the murder of Skip Lombardi." Lane looked out the window. A male cyclist in a yellow jersey leaned his bike up against the iron fence. He bent to lock his bike. The yellow was stained with green on one shoulder.

"So far, that's what we've got." Harper looked out the window.

A second cyclist arrived. He was wearing black lycra shorts, a black jersey, and black helmet. There was a pinecone sticking out at an angle in the top vent of his helmet.

The cyclist in the yellow jersey stood up and turned to face the other.

Lane stood up. "We'd better go outside."

Yellow jersey threw a punch. It connected with the black helmet of the other rider. The pinecone popped out. The cyclists wrapped each other up, fell over the fence, and onto the table, where the startled couple fell to the ground.

The waiter said, "Hey!"

Lane was first out the door. The cyclists rolled in opposite directions and stood. Lane pulled out his ID and kept his voice low. "Hello, gentlemen." The combatants had to listen carefully to hear his voice.

Harper pulled out his identification and stood next to the yellow cyclist.

"I think she's done something to her shoulder." The man at the table crouched over the woman, who was holding her arm and crying. There was blood on the front of her white T-shirt.

Harper nodded at Lane. He went to the woman. Her face was pale and she was shaking. "Better get her to emergency. She's going into shock." He pulled his phone out of his pocket and dialled. He got up and walked toward the cyclists.

Lane pulled out a pair of handcuffs with his free hand.

Harper did the same.

The cyclist in black started to run. Harper grabbed his wrist and twisted it up between the cyclist's shoulder blades. Harper cuffed one hand and then the other. He kept the phone tucked up against his shoulder and ear.

Lane walked over to the second cyclist and, using one hand, cuffed him.

"Not my fault," the black-outfitted cyclist said.

Lane and Harper sat the pair down at opposite ends of the terrace.

The ambulance arrived five minutes later, just after the first police cruiser.

The injured woman was loaded into the ambulance. Her husband followed in their car. As he pulled away, he looked at the pair of cyclists. Lane saw murder in the husband's eyes.

The cyclists were loaded into separate cruisers.

When Lane and Harper got back inside, their coffees were full and hot. The waiter said, "Thanks guys."

"How often does that happen?" Harper asked.

"Every now and then, cyclists or joggers get aggressive." The waiter took their cold coffees away.

Lane looked out the window. Another waiter picked up chairs and began mopping up the coffee that had spilled over the bricks. Lane thought about the adrenaline rush resulting from the aftermath of the fight, and he thought about the husband, whose wife was at the hospital.

Harper said, "What?"

"Bystanders. We've been looking too close to home on this one. What did you say the name of Alex's friend was?" Lane turned back to Harper.

"Aidan."

"We need to talk with her, and we need to talk with Norm some more." Lane took a sip of coffee. "Remember what Eva said when we asked who was a good shot?"

Harper nodded. "She changed the subject."

"This wasn't what I had in mind when I asked for a different outfit." Alex the marionette wore a white shirt with a series of red circles on the front and the back. He also wore black jeans and shoes.

Aidan shook her marionette head. "You're never satisfied, are you?"

"It's just that I never wore anything like this either." Alex looked out in the direction of where the audience would be. "Anybody got a mirror?"

"That's the point. You're dead, so you shouldn't wear what you wore when you were alive." Aidan peered offstage. Both Aidans wore blue jeans and blue satin shirts. Their belts were white with silver belt buckles the size of dessert plates. They wore red cowboy boots and white hats.

Alex turned to Aidan. "There's nobody out there."

"Not yet." She tipped her hat back and put her thumbs in her belt.

Alex imitated a drawl. "You doin' one of those 'merican themes? I mean it's red, white, and blue all over y'all."

"I just like the colours. It's not a political statement." Aidan adopted a coquettish pose. "Well, maybe just a bit of one."

"That's what I thought. There isn't one thing here you haven't done for a reason." Alex used an extended right hand to indicate the stage, props, and costumes.

"Glad you noticed."

"And you're still keeping the big secret even from me?" Alex pointed at a closed box on stage right. All of the other boxes were open to reveal hanging marionettes and backdrops.

"You need to be surprised when you see it. It's the finale. You'll understand when we come to the end of the show on Saturday." Aidan walked over to the closed wooden box and stood in front with her arms crossed.

"Perhaps." Alex adopted a thoughtful pose. "This outfit was an unpleasant surprise. Hopefully whatever's in the box will be a pleasant one." He moved closer to the closed box, peering around one side and then the other.

"Is my grandmother going to be out there?" Alex looked offstage.

"Called her today. Says she wouldn't miss it." Aidan leaned back against the box as Alex continued to study it.

"Norm too?" Alex started to dance. He leaned on one foot and then the other, doing figure eights in front of Aidan. He danced around the middle of the stage, hovering and swooping.

"Hasn't made up his mind yet." Aidan watched Alex with suspicion.

"He still looking out for you and Eva?" Alex held his elbows out level with his shoulders.

"Yep. He thinks he's doing what his mom told him to do, keeping *us* safe when really it's supposed to be the other way around."

"Can't wait to hear what they have to say. I mean Eva's never been to a rodeo quite like this one." Alex stretched his arms into wings and continued his dance.

"You worried about it?" Aidan leaned against the wall and crossed one leg in front of the other.

"A little bit. I mean, she and I never really talked about it." Alex looked sideways at Aidan.

"Give her some credit. She's one smart woman. She learned sign language when she found out you were deaf." Aidan studied Alex.

"Being deaf is different from being … well, you know, some people think it's a choice."

"This isn't like you. Having second thoughts?" Aidan added laughter to her voice.

"Maybe. I'm worried." Alex stopped dancing, looked at Aidan.

"Worried about what?" Aidan uncrossed her legs and leaned forward.

"I feel a storm coming and it's headed your way." Alex hung his head.

"You worry too much." Aidan punched Alex's shoulder.

Alex laughed. "Now that's a switch."

ch*a*pter 14

"Amanda. It's Amanda." Christine said the words like the name should mean something.

Lane looked at Amanda standing in the kitchen. She was the same height as Christine. Amanda's hair was dyed black, her eyes were blue, and she had the face of an angel with pierced eyebrows. She wore a leather jacket, knee-length shorts, canvas running shoes, and a black T-shirt. Lane held out his hand and thought, *Is she moving in too?*

Amanda pushed his hand away and hugged Lane around the waist. He looked at Christine for help. Matt leaned against the fridge with his arms crossed.

Amanda said, "You don't remember me?"

Lane recognized something in her voice. "You mean Amanda? Mandy? My brother's daughter?" Lane hugged her back.

"You do remember! I didn't forget you. Even when they stopped talking about you, I remembered. You sent me birthday cards every year."

"You used to lick your finger and stick it in my ..." Lane got chills up his spine.

Amanda stuck a wet index finger in his ear.

Matt bent double with laughter.

Christine said, "She still does."

"Are you staying for dinner?" Arthur asked.

They moved to the deck while Roz chased wasps and made endless rounds of the spruce tree.

"I can't really remember when it happened or why. My parents just stopped talking about you. There were no more Christmas dinners. No more birthdays with you. Remember the barbecues in the summer? It all just stopped." Amanda looked around the table. No one replied. She looked at Lane. "Do you remember it that way?"

"Yes." Lane watched Roz while thinking about Riley in their old yard.

Arthur set a salad bowl in the middle of the table. "He was told to stay away. There were several phone calls from his brother telling him that Lane had made his choice, and they were making their choice. By that time, Lane and I were living together. I was there when the calls came in. It was like a death."

Lane got up to check the chicken on the barbecue. He felt emotions beginning to boil over.

"My mom went along with it?" Christine asked.

At the opening of the barbecue lid, Roz roared onto the deck and skidded to a halt next to Lane.

"What's going on? Anybody been feeding the dog from the table?" Lane thought, *What am I so upset about? I've dealt with this. I like this life better than the old one.* He looked back at Matt, Arthur, Christine, and Amanda. Only Amanda made eye contact.

Roz's tail was a windshield wiper on the deck. Her tongue hung out. Her pleading eyes never left Lane.

"Well, did my mom go along with the 'excommunication' or didn't she?" Christine asked.

"We didn't hear from any of them. Lane was told he wasn't supposed to be around his nieces and nephews." Arthur held up the bottle of white wine. "Anyone?"

"Me, please." Amanda held up her glass.

Arthur smiled. "You're underage." He looked at Lane.

Lane shrugged. "Anyone driving?" He worked to keep his voice low, conversational, even though he felt like screaming at the outrage of losing all those years.

They all shook their heads.

Arthur poured five glasses.

Lane picked up the platter from the table. It took all of his concentration to take the chicken off the barbecue.

Matt passed the salad.

"So you were cut off from us, and no one asked us what we thought?" Amanda scooped Greek salad.

"I guess so." Lane looked to his left. Roz was there, sitting and waiting. He saw Riley again, head resting on his paws.

"How come you don't say much, Uncle Lane?" Matt asked.

Lane looked across the table at his nephew. Lane's words flew out before he took the time to think about them. "You know what it's like! You're cut off from your family! My family wanted nothing more to do with me! They preached about the truth! When I told them the truth, when I came out, they disowned me. It was all very polite, of course! They just stopped inviting me over! I'd call, but my calls would never be returned, or they didn't have time to talk! I finally gave up after I was told I was a bad influence around my nieces and nephews!"

Matt leaned back, a bit shocked at the explosion he'd sparked.

Lane read his nephew's expression. "I'm not mad at you. I thought I was over it. I was wrong."

"Finally, it's out!" Arthur put his arms up like someone had just scored a goal.

Lane opened his mouth and closed it.

Matt smiled. "So, it's just a mask! You always act like you're in control. But, you're just like the rest of us!" He started to laugh.

Roz rubbed her cheek against Lane's knee.

Christine started to chuckle. "The dog's already figured you out! You're just a teddy bear on the inside."

Amanda sawed at her chicken breast. Half the breast shot across the table and ended up on Arthur's plate.

Arthur looked at her with amazement. As they laughed, the dog began to howl.

After supper, dishes, and a second bottle of wine, they stayed outside. Roz lay next to Lane. He felt her nose against his hand. He rubbed the thick fur on the back of her neck. When he pulled his hand away, she sat up and poked him with her nose until he returned to scratching her.

Lane felt the wine loosening his tongue and looked at the pink sky silhouetting the mountains.

"It's great to be able to see the mountains," Amanda said. "We can't see them from my house."

"That's one of the reasons why we bought this place." Arthur sat opposite from Lane.

"New house, new dog, new family." Lane was surprised as anyone at what he'd said.

"Is that why you didn't want us to get a dog, after what happened to Riley and what happened to your family?" Matt asked.

Lane thought for a moment. "Maybe. You get close and then ..."

"Tell me about it. I know exactly what you mean." Christine lifted her glass to look at the sunset through the wine.

"It's always about you. You never think of anyone else, do you?" Matt glared at Christine.

Amanda laughed. "You two really are like brother and sister. Always bickering. Just like me and my brothers. Always reading more into what's said than is actually there."

"And sticking up for one another. Like after the dance." Arthur lifted his glass and drained it.

"Did she tell you?" Matt looked sideways at Christine.

"Christine didn't tell us anything. We have eyes. We could see what was going on. She had your back," Lane said.

"Oh, I forgot. You're a detective." Matt looked for Roz who wagged her tail, put her paws on the arm of his chair and licked his face.

"Don't get mad at Uncle Lane! He didn't do anything!" Christine said.

Roz moved to Christine and licked her face.

"See what I mean?" Amanda raised her wine to see what was so interesting about the sunset, then she looked through the glass at Matt and Christine.

"I do." Lane raised his glass and saw the pinks of the sunset accented by the legs of white wine in his glass and thought, *Things just never turn out the way you expect them to.*

The phone rang.

Christine got up and went inside. A few seconds later, she poked her head out the back door. "It's for you, Uncle Lane."

Lane got up and went into the kitchen. *It must be ten degrees warmer in here,* he thought. "Hello."

"It's me," Harper said.

"What's up?" Lane sat down.

"Christine tells me the party is going well."

"It has its ups and downs."

"She says you're getting a little wild and crazy." Harper sounded pleased.

"A little bit."

"The DNA results are in."

"And?"

"Lombardi's blood and hair are a match. It looks like Blake killed him. And Rosco, the dog, was a match as well."

Lane thought for a moment. "So the most reasonable conclusion is that Blake killed Lombardi and then the dog."

"You think the dog tried to protect Lombardi?" Harper asked.

"Probably."

THURSDAY, JULY 11

chapter 15

"We need to talk with Norm, Eva, and Aidan." Lane watched as the houses abruptly ended and fields opened up. The further they travelled, the more horses they would see. The last time, he'd seen a pair of colts racing side by side along a fence line. Lane thought, *I hope they're out again.*

"There's a coyote." Harper pointed to his side of the highway.

Lane looked to his left.

The coyote was the colour of sage. It trotted along the shoulder before darting into the ditch and disappearing into some brush.

"Wanna stop at the gas station?" Harper asked.

"Good idea. Everybody needs fuel. It's a good place

to find out what's going on around here." Lane spotted the Super Service station sign. The fifties architecture was becoming avant-garde. The reliance on metal, glass, and stucco had preserved the structure for more than half a century. A fresh coat of white paint and green trim had done the rest. It was becoming a Mecca for the workers and residents of the new development across the highway and down the road.

They pulled up and parked on the east side of the station. Lane spotted a couple near the outdoor freezer. The eyes of the teenaged boy met Lane's. To the detective, the boy's eyes were the epitome of boredom. The girl was a second skin wrapped around the boy. Lane couldn't see the back of her head, but it looked like she was working on leaving her brand on the boy's neck.

Lane looked down. The boy had his knee between her legs. She moved back and forth, rubbing her jeans up against his.

Harper held the door open. "Coming?"

Lane smiled at the joke and walked through the door.

Harper followed.

The man behind the counter was somewhere between forty and sixty. He had the bread-dough complexion of a smoker and a belly stretching the fabric of his wine-coloured golf shirt.

Harper headed for the coffee. "Want one?"

"Sure." Lane kept his eyes on the man behind the counter, who returned Lane's stare.

"Cream and sugar?" Harper asked.

"Yes, please."

Lane read "Al" on the man's nametag and the gold chain around his neck. It was attached to a predatory bird the size of a luxury car's hood ornament. The words "Golden Eagle" hung from the talons of the bird.

"You're the police?" Al asked.

Lane nodded.

"You're the ones who came and asked my daughter all those questions?"

"That's correct." Lane decided to keep his answers short and to the point.

"What do you want besides a cup of coffee?" Al glanced out the window.

It looked to Lane as if Al were keeping an eye on the make-out couple reflected in the curved mirror hanging above the pumps. Lane glanced at the poster of the cowboy on the wall.

"Who do you talk to if you want to get rid of some gophers?" Lane asked.

"Why don't you just come out with it? You want to know who's a good shot around here." Al challenged Lane with his eyes. "I'm not stupid just because I live out in the country."

Harper brought the coffees to the counter. "It would save a lot of time if you would tell us."

Lane pulled out a ten dollar bill and handed it to Al.

Al took the ten, opened the cash register and handed Lane the change.

Al said, "Have a nice day."

"Who's a good shot around here?" Harper asked.

"Everyone knew Blake and his boys ran Alex down. The problem was, no one could prove it. Now Blake and his boys are dead. As far as I'm concerned, that's the end of the story. Diggin' deeper into this'll only get people riled up again. You have no idea what people around here'll do when they get riled." Al closed the cash register. "You gentleman have a nice day."

Harper started to say more.

Lane smiled and nodded in the direction of the door. He took the coffees from Harper and backed out the door. Lane walked over to the couple making out near the freezer. The boy's eyes studied Lane.

"Do like your coffee black or with cream and sugar?" Lane walked closer to the couple.

The girl turned her round, heavily made-up face to Lane. She said, "I take mine black. He likes cream and sugar."

Lane handed them each a cup. They watched him warily.

Lane stepped back a metre. "Who's the best shot around here?"

The girl and boy looked at one another, surprised by the question. The girl said, "I think his name is Norm. Drives around on an ATV. Lives up there. Close to T'suu T'ina." She pointed toward the mountains.

"Thanks." Lane walked to the car. Harper followed.

Inside the car, Harper hesitated before turning the key. "So, who do we see first?"

"Eva. She'll know where Norm is." Lane put his seat belt on.

Harper turned the key and shifted into drive. He tried to joke, but the words came out all wrong. "Better get the vests out, then."

Eva was in the yard. She was moving three sections of garden hose to the next tree in Alex's remembrance grove. She put her hand over her eyebrows to shade out the sun. When she recognized the car, Lane and Harper, she waved them over. A pair of hummingbirds whizzed past her.

"How come Norm's ATV is parked inside the Quonset?" Harper asked as he turned the car around so they could escape easily if it came to that.

Lane took a long look around. He thought, *If it isn't safe, it isn't safe in the car either.* He opened his door.

Harper waited before turning off the engine.

Lane walked toward Eva, who bent to set the hose under one of the trees. Her hand went to her right knee. She used her hand to help push herself back up.

Lane heard the car engine stop. Harper's door opened. Lane did not turn.

Eva walked toward Lane. She neither smiled nor frowned.

Lane saw that she wore running shoes, a T-shirt, and blue jeans. There was mud on her knees.

He looked beyond and around her. Harper was moving to his left; Lane could hear his partner.

Eva said, "Norm's at the rodeo. Drove him there this morning. That's why you're here."

"How did you know?" Lane asked.

"Got a phone call from Al at the Super Service. Told me you were asking questions about who's the best shot around here." Eva stood in front of Lane.

Lane heard Harper moving closer.

"Where does he live?" Harper asked.

"South and west of here. About three kilometres." Eva crossed her arms under her breasts. "Go a little further down the road and turn right. Last house on that road. It's white. Potato garden on the side closest to the road."

"How come he went to the rodeo?" Lane watched the way Harper kept looking at the evergreen trees Eva was watering.

"To help Aidan. Coffee?"

Lane and Harper looked at one another. They looked around the yard.

"There'll be no more shootin'. No reason for it." Eva walked toward the house.

"Okay." Harper followed.

Lane stood on the step as a hummingbird swooped past, stopped near a honeysuckle blossom, and hovered there. Another hummingbird swooped in and attacked the first. Both flew away.

Inside, they took off their shoes while Eva measured water and coffee. "Norm took all the muffins with him. Aidan asked for them special."

Lane sat down at the table.

Harper watched while Eva fished out coffee cups. He looked at Lane and nodded in Eva's direction. Lane turned as Eva closed the cupboard door.

Eva finished with the coffee maker and reached into the fridge for milk. She brought the milk and sugar to the table. "Got more questions?"

"I've always got lots of those." Lane smiled.

Eva did the same. "Aidan and Norm are my family."

"I understand," Lane said.

"You do?" Eva watched him with an intensity that made Harper shift uncomfortably.

"Yes. Just because they're not your own doesn't mean they're not your family."

Eva frowned. "Maybe you do understand. Everything is even up now. The boys who killed my grandson are dead. Blake Rogers would have killed you but he's dead. What good does it do to find out the rest?"

Eva poured three cups of coffee and sat down at the table. She sipped her coffee, waiting for Lane and Harper to do the same.

Lane lifted his cup then set it down. He decided that to leave anything unsaid would amount to lying, and she would sense it. "We got a match on the bullet that killed Blake Rogers. It came from the same weapon that wounded me."

Eva was silent for a moment. "You and your law. My grandson was killed. Everyone knew who did it. No one could prove it. The boys who killed him disappeared or were killed. And Blake Rogers would have killed you." She pointed at both of them. "Rogers was killed to save the both of you. Everything is even now. Your law won't change that."

Harper put his cup down. "We know about the land claim. We think that's why Blake Rogers killed Alex. Still, we need to know who killed Rogers."

"And what good will that do? Who will be helped by this knowledge?" Eva watched Harper closely.

Harper waited for Lane.

Lane looked at Eva. "The families of the missing men will want to know where they are. We need to talk with Norm, and we need to talk with Aidan."

"They're at the rodeo." Eva stated the fact in a tone as flat as the prairies to the east.

"The rodeo hasn't started yet," Harper said.

"Practicin'. Gettin' her show ready."

Lane looked at her. "The rodeo's a big place."

"Not that big," Eva said.

Five minutes later, inside the car, Harper said, "Eva hates guns, right?"

"Yes. She said that." Lane did up his seat belt.

"Then how come she has three boxes of .22 shells and a bolt action in the same cupboard as her coffee cups?"

Lane leaned on the concrete half-wall of the walkway joining the Saddledome arena and the Roundup Centre where graduations and business shows were held at the Stampede Grounds. He looked over at the Big Four building, then across the parking lot to the back side of the grandstand where fans watched rodeo events every July.

"We've checked it all." Harper leaned against a pillar.

"Eva doesn't lie," Lane said.

"Then Aidan and Norm must be hiding." Harper yawned.

"Or we're looking in the wrong place." Lane watched a white stretch limousine pull up in front of the Roundup Centre. A girl in a prom dress poked her head out of the sun roof.

Harper turned and looked north. A black cloud moved east across the northern edge of the city. "Looks like someone's getting rain."

Aidan crouched atop the set and manipulated Alex's strings. They were inside the barn. It was filled with the musty scent of hay and mud. Rain pattered against the roof and windows.

"We've got an audience! Hey Norm!" Alex waved.

Norm waved once and crossed his arms. He sat in front of them on a lawn chair.

"Good to see you again." Alex moved to the edge of the stage.

Norm nodded and leaned back in his lawn chair. He hitched his thumbs in his empty gun belt. "Yep."

"Come to see me or the show?" Alex moved to sit in a rocking chair and crossed one leg over the other.

"Both." Norm leaned forward, studying the marionette.

"I heard there's been some excitement around my grandmother's place." Alex rocked back.

"Them boys that run you down. Well, they won't be botherin' nobody else, Alex." Norm took off his tan cowboy hat, revealing the scar along his forehead. He looked out the window at the rain.

"That's good to know."

"I saw 'em do it, you know." Norm hooked the cap over his right knee and looked at Alex.

"What?" Alex stopped rocking.

"Saw 'em run you down like a dog. Saw 'em from the edge of the trees. Watched 'em drive by. Recognized the four of 'em."

Alex stood up. "How come you never told anyone?"

Norm pointed at his chest. "Who's gonna believe

me? Besides, when I went to Eva's she was cryin', Aidan was cryin', and I was cryin'. Alex, the words just wouldn't come out."

"Did you get the license?" Alex asked.

"Can't read. You know that. But I knew who it was. That's why." He looked out the window.

"Why?" Aidan looked away from her marionettes.

"Why I kept planting those trees for you." Norm looked at the floor. "My mom told me to look after you."

"Thank you, Norm," Alex said.

"You were good to me, Alex. Did what I could. Yep. Did what I should to be good right back." Norm looked off to the right.

"What did you do, Norm?" Alex asked.

"Planted them trees for you."

"What's that mean?" Alex looked over his shoulder and up at Aidan.

"You planted a tree every year. And after you died …" Norm pointed a finger at his chest. "… I kept that up for you. It's what Mother woulda wanted."

SATURDAY, JULY 13

ch*a*pter 16

"You're treating Roz like she's a doll. She hates that!" Matt's voice carried from the deck to the kitchen where Arthur and Lane sat drinking coffee. Lane got up and peered through a clear diamond in the back-door window. Christine hugged Roz and glared at Matt. Roz displayed nearly all of her teeth in a decidedly unfriendly smile as she licked her lips.

"Do you really think we should go? I mean those two have been at it since they got up." Arthur sounded worried.

Lane sat down. "There's more room for them to argue at the rodeo. It's better than having them around the house and fighting. So my vote is we go. We've promised Glenn we'll be there, and Harper will be a little less uncomfortable if we're there."

The argument between Christine and Matt got louder.

"What have you got against me anyway?" Christine said.

"Nothin'," Matt said.

"That's no answer. You've been mad at me since I got here!"

Lane and Arthur couldn't help but listen.

"You've still got a mom and you left her! Mine's dead, and my father doesn't want me anymore! You leave your mom and come here just when it's starting to feel like home for me!" Matt's voice choked off the last word.

Christine started off in a matter-of-fact tone. "My mom didn't want me. She wouldn't talk to me for a month before I left. Most of the people there wouldn't talk to me. Those who did only talked to me when no one else was around! My mom didn't want me around any more. I was an embarrassment."

Matt sniffed before he spoke. "How could you think that? Mothers aren't like that!"

"Maybe your mother wasn't, but mine was. Look at me! I was an embarrassment. Look!" There was a pause before Christine said, "All of Paradise was white. I was the only one whose skin was a different colour. Nobody said anything, but after a while you could just tell. They didn't want me there. And after a while, my mother started to act the same way. She kept telling me to wear a hat in the summer so I wouldn't get a tan. She was ashamed of my skin! Like it was my choice!"

Arthur and Lane had to listen closely when Matt spoke. The boy's voice was low, almost a whisper.

Matt cleared his throat. "My dad never went anywhere with me. Never went to one of my games. Never went to my school for interviews. He always found an excuse for not being there. I embarrassed him."

"How did you know?" Christine asked.

"I just knew like you knew about your mom and the people in Paradise. Some things you just know."

Christine asked, "So why are you here?"

"Uncle Arthur and Uncle Lane like having me around. And I can tell, they feel the same way about you. I guess I'm jealous."

No one dared speak.

The quiet stretched out until Arthur went to the back door and said, "Come on you two, it's time to go." He held the door open until Christine and Matt came inside.

An angry rumble shook the windows.

"What was that?" Arthur asked.

"Thunder," Matt said.

"Come on. It's time to load up the Jeep," Lane said.

They travelled in rain and silence for the half hour it took to drive north and east along the top edge of the city past houses, malls, and a couple of golf courses. They turned north and the city ended. Less than five minutes later, they eased through the gates of Symon's Valley Ranch. They parked on the grass behind one of the washrooms.

Christine opened her door. "Looks like the rain's finished."

The sky to the west was blue and clear. The trailing edge of the storm moved east.

Arthur smiled. "The infield will be muddy. This should be lots of fun."

They carried lawn chairs and dodged puddles as they walked past trailers and motor homes on their way to the infield. Lane thought of the right thing to say to Christine and Matt before deciding to say nothing.

"What's that?" Christine pointed at a tiny corral with balloons and blowup love dolls leaning up against rough-sawn fence boards.

Arthur read the sign. "Heavy petting zoo."

"It's a bar, I think," Lane said too quickly.

They found a spot on the sloped grass at the southeast corner, in front of the stands, in behind the steel fence and to one side of the bleachers. The sun shone on a muddy infield. Its soil had taken on the consistency of canned soup.

Two pairs of contestants ran from the far side to near the fence in front of Lane, Arthur, and the kids. Each pair headed for a tethered goat. One man grabbed and lifted the hind end of the goat so his partner could guide the goat's back legs through a pair of white panties. The other goat managed to evade the competitors. One man tripped over the rope and fell face first into the mud. Laughter washed over the infield.

Christine looked at the infield and the crowd. Couples and groups wore cowboy hats and ball caps. She looked at Lane. He held out a twenty dollar bill. "Just in case you want to get something to eat or drink."

"Thanks," Christine said.

Arthur handed another twenty to Matt.

"There you are!"

They turned to see Erinn carrying Jessica, followed by Harper and Glenn who were weighed down with chairs and bags stuffed to overflowing with baby supplies.

"We miss anything?" Glenn asked as he unfolded two chairs and sat next to Matt.

"No. They're still trying to put panties on the goats," Matt smiled.

"Hi Christine. Ready for some fun?" Erinn sat down with Jessica in the chair next to Christine.

"I think so," Christine said.

"I know how you feel. Last year was my first at the rodeo. Lane and Arthur brought me. I sat around feeling like a minority. You know, a breeder in a strange land." Erinn smiled at Lane, Harper and Matt.

"A breeder?" Christine asked.

"I'm a breeder. You know, a straight married woman with children." Erinn smiled. "It helps to know the lingo. What's going on here? All these long faces!"

"Christine and I were fighting," Matt said.

"So? What family doesn't?" Erinn said.

The announcer said, "There'll be a short intermission while we prepare for our next event."

"Should be the drag queens," Arthur said.

"We're just in time, then," Erinn said.

Glenn walked over to Christine. "Come on. Let's go take a look around."

"I don't know," Christine said.

Glenn pulled her up and out of the chair. "You too, Matt."

"What's new?" Harper sat down next to Arthur after the kids left.

Jessica began to cry.

Harper stood up and picked up his daughter. Erinn smiled as Harper walked back and forth behind them, rocking their daughter. He said, "How's my Jessica?" She gradually stopped crying.

"Daddy's girl." Erinn looked at Lane. "Well?"

Lane said, "Matt's been rejected by his dad and Christine by her mom. Now they're living with us and fighting with each other."

"Did you talk with them?" Erinn asked.

Lane and Arthur looked at each other. "About what?" they said in stereo.

"I don't know. The future?" Erinn rolled her eyes. "They've got nowhere to go and have been rejected by people who shouldn't ever reject them. You two know anything about rejection?" Erinn tried to keep a straight face.

Lane thought, *Oh, shit.*

Arthur said, "You've got to be kidding?"

"Glenn figured it was only a matter of time before we rejected him." Harper sat down. Jessica started to cry. He got up and started to walk with her.

"So, what did you do?" Arthur asked.

"We talked." Erinn looked left as the corral gate opened. "Told him that we wanted him around. After a while, he believed us."

The announcer said, "For our next event …" His voice was drowned by the roar of cheers and applause from the spectators.

Three drag queens waved at the crowd. They all wore metallic-blue beehive hair. Each wore a sequined blue dress, black pantyhose, and white rubber boots. And all three wore conical bras that came to sharp points. Each of the queens was followed by attendants in coveralls dyed different shades of the rainbow.

"Wow!" Erinn said.

"We're back!" Glenn sat down with a brown paper shopping bag filled with popcorn.

"What's this?" Christine pointed at the corral.

No one answered as the three stars waded through the infield's ankle-deep mud. The buzzer sounded. One calf was let out of an enclosure. Two attendants grabbed for the rope around the calf's neck. The calf struggled as they dragged and pushed it over to the first queen. He revealed red satin panties as he straddled the calf. The crowd cheered while the attendants pushed and pulled the calf and queen across a line on the far side of the corral.

"Well, that looked easy!" the announcer said.

The next pair of attendants got ready. The gate opened. The calf launched itself. The first attendant was knocked flat by the calf. The second grabbed for the rope and missed. The drag queen high-stepped his way closer to the calf, managed to grab the rope, and was dragged across the infield. The queen's paired V cups acted as hydroplanes, cutting parallel wakes in the mud. The queen hung on. Mud coated his face, hair, and mustache. He let go, slid to a stop, and rolled onto his back. The crowd cheered and clapped as the queen stood. He tried to flick the mud off his hands before righting his hair.

"I've never seen anything like this," Christine said.

"It's only getting started," Glenn said.

They watched various events for another hour while the sun gradually dried out the infield. The final event was bull riding. Riders in flack jackets rode bulls while the clown picked cowpokes out of the mud after they dismounted or were thrown.

After the last event, Matt asked, "Are we going out for supper?"

Jessica started to cry.

"We've got tickets for dinner here. We'll just wait for Jessica," Arthur said.

Erinn pulled a blanket over her shoulders and began to breastfeed.

Christine looked uneasily at the crowd. One cowboy kissed another. Two cowgirls held muddy hands.

"Don't worry, it's not a disease you catch." Glenn put his hand on Christine's shoulder.

Christine looked back at him, shocked that he'd read her mind.

The announcer said, "Dinner's on! Don't miss the best beef and bison you're gonna find anywhere. It's at the Wagon Wheel Hall. There are still a few tickets left, so hurry up. And for your added pleasure we've got a show called *Wingin' It.* This is the debut of an incredibly talented local puppeteer and artist."

"Go on ahead," Erinn said.

"We'll wait." Arthur turned to Matt and Christine. "You know we want both of you to stay with us." Arthur pulled Lane closer.

Lane heard the sudden and complete silence surrounding them as Christine and Matt watched their uncles.

Lane thought, *Say something! Say the right thing!* "We do. I think of us as family now. I know we're not your real parents, but we're here and we want you both around. Permanently."

Matt looked at the ground.

Erinn sniffed.

Glenn smiled.

Christine moved to Lane and hugged him around the neck before turning to Arthur and wiping the back of her hand across his cheek.

For a full minute all Lane could hear was the sound of Jessica sucking on Erinn's breast.

Forty minutes later, they stood in line out front of the Wagon Wheel Hall.

Harper patted Jessica's back to work out any gas. The baby rewarded him with a satisfied belch.

Matt closed his eyes. "Man, that smells good."

Jessica farted.

Matt looked at Harper and smiled. "I meant the food."

They stood behind one of the cowgirls who was covered in drying mud.

As they entered the open-air eating area with its

picnic tables, there was an unusual quiet. Lane looked at the woman on stage who was dressed in red cowboy boots, blue jeans, and a blue satin shirt. Lane stared at the white-hatted marionette who was dressed exactly like the puppeteer working the strings.

The other marionette wore jeans, black shoes, and a white shirt with targets painted in red on the front and back. He stood alone at the front of the stage.

"Alex!" the female marionette gestured with her hands. The puppeteer suspended the marionette from a metal hook. Her head hung in grief.

The puppeteer lifted a white pickup truck. It had "Republic of Alberta" painted in black across its side. Inside were four heads with cowboy hats. As the truck swung down, one of its doors opened. The marionette with the target painted on his shirt was sent flying off the stage. When the truck reached the top of its arc, the puppeteer grabbed it and set it down behind the stage.

The puppeteer opened a door in one of the wooden chests and out walked a duplicate of Alex's marionette with the targets on its back and chest. "And that was that. One deaf and gay First Nations man killed on the side of the highway. Aidan never forgave herself." Alex looked up at the puppeteer and then at Aidan the marionette.

Lane felt his attention shift from puppeteer to the marionettes. At that moment, the marionettes became real to him. He listened to them, watched them the way he would listen to any other living, breathing person.

Aidan's head lifted. "I should have done something." The marionette's head dropped.

Alex turned to her. "There was nothing you could have done. After that, I was a star. The Premier even had a name for me."

The Premier stepped out of the closet. His over-sized face was mostly jowls and nose.

Alex said, "Hey, Mr. Premier."

The Premier wore a headdress and pinstriped suit. "Where's the parade? I need to get out in front of it!"

The audience began to laugh. One man said, "You're not leading the pride parade!"

The Premier turned to walk back into the closet.

"Wait! I've got a question." Alex moved closer to the Premier.

The Premier turned to face Alex. "I don't have to talk to you. You're a ghost."

"Spirit."

"There's a difference?" the Premier asked.

"Big difference. I always wanted to ask you why you called me the 'victim of the week'?"

The Premier said, "It was a slow news week. The media needed an issue, and you got your fifteen minutes of fame. I had to put a spin on the story. Nothing personal."

"You're wrong. Murder is very, very personal." Alex moved closer.

"Is that a pie in your hand?" the Premier asked as he backed away.

The Premier's headdress was lifted off. He turned so the audience could read the licence plate on the back of his suit jacket.

"What's it say?" The Premier looked back over his shoulder.

Alex moved the side of the stage.

"What's it say?" the Premier asked.

The license plate had an "I", a heart, a number two, a shovel, a silhouette of the province, and a bull.

Someone in the audience said, "I love to shovel Alberta bullshit!"

"That's right!" someone else said. There was laughter and an enthusiastic round of applause.

The Premier went back into his closet.

Alex faced the audience. "There were witnesses, but there was no proof. The hit and run happened too fast. I was buried near a tree on my grandmother's acreage. It was against the law, but my grandmother has a way of doing what she wants. She plants honeysuckle over my grave every summer and the hummingbirds come."

Aidan the marionette lifted her head. She moved forward and stood beside Alex. "The case is still open. We plant a tree every year to celebrate Alex's life. And every once in a while he can dance."

Aidan stepped back. A door opened in the side of the closed case. It was Alex dressed in white, red, and green. There were moccasins on his feet and feathers at his back. His eyes were circled with red.

Alex looked up at Aidan the puppeteer. "So this is your big secret. This is your gift!" Alex the dancer stood at centre stage. Alex the target stepped into the background. The puppeteer hung him from a hook.

A drumbeat began in the corner. Lane looked across the room as the chanting began. Four men sat around the drum and beat as one heart. He looked back to the stage.

A white ceramic flower stood at the centre of the stage. It was almost as tall as Alex's marionette.

Alex said, "I can't hear the drum, but I can feel it!" He pointed at his heart and bent at the waist to begin his dance. "Even death cannot stop me from dancing!" He circled the flower and backed away, spun, then returned to the flower. After he stuck his nose close to the flower, he appeared to hover, moving his arms so fast they became a blur of green. Then he repeated the motions, dancing around the flower. With each pass, his speed increased until the separate colours blurred into a rainbow.

Applause erupted from the audience.

The stage disappeared in front of Lane as the audience stood to clap and cheer.

Someone nearby shouted at the puppeteer, "Who makes your outfits?"

The chanting and the drum carried on.

Someone said, "Drag king!"

Another person picked it up. "Drag king!"

The crowd began to chant to the beat of the drums. "DRAG KING! DRAG KING!"

The puppeteer stood above the crowd. Her eyes focused on someone to Lane's right. Lane looked and saw Harper who nodded his head at her and smiled.

The puppeteer bowed to the audience and as she did, she lifted Alex. Suspended in midair, he bent low at the waist; then his right arm swept forward in a midair bow. There was a roar from the crowd. The puppeteer waited for the applause to slow before looking at Alex's marionette. "I've been so angry with you. If you could dance like that, why couldn't you dance out of the way of the truck?"

After the show, Glenn drove everyone but Lane and Harper home. They waited for the puppeteer, who appeared in a nondescript red ball cap, blue jeans, and white shirt.

"Aidan, do you want some help to load up?" Harper smiled.

Aidan looked at him. "You the one who got shot?"

"That was him." Harper pointed at Lane. "I just got shot at."

Lane waited.

"I could use some help. But you two aren't here just to help me get packed up." Aidan lifted her hat and wiped sweat away from her forehead with her sleeve.

"There are still two men missing." Lane lifted the end of one case.

Aidan looked at each of them in turn. "I'll pull the truck around. We'll load up, then we'll talk."

"What about supper? You must be hungry." Harper picked up the other end of the case.

"Supper would be nice. Thanks." Aidan went to get the truck.

While they waited in line to pick up Aidan's dinner, Lane said, "Eva told us Aidan was at the rodeo. We just assumed she meant the Stampede."

By the time she returned, Lane and Harper had all the cases waiting outside the entrance to the Wagon Wheel Hall. Everything was loaded up five minutes later.

Lane handed her the plate he'd set on the hood of the pickup. "Here's supper."

Aidan looked at him for a moment before accepting the food. She sat on the open tailgate. Aidan used a plastic fork to scoop up beans, spear salad, and pick up slices of bison. She mopped up the remaining sauce with a bun.

Harper leaned against the fender and Lane sat on the tailgate.

Aidan let out a long sigh. "I've been too nervous to eat."

Lane watched her walk over and put the plate in a garbage can.

Harper said, "The show was magnificent."

"I wasn't sure how people would react." Aidan smiled and looked away.

"Did you get your answer?" Lane asked.

She sat on the tailgate. "Yes."

"Was it worth it?" Harper leaned his elbows on the sides of the pickup's box.

"You bet." Aidan pulled her knees up and rested her chin on them.

She's exhausted, Lane thought. "We have some questions."

Aidan cocked her head sideways to look at him. She leaned her cheek on her knees. "Of course."

"How long have you been here?" Harper asked.

"Since you last saw me. And I can't prove I was always here. I was rehearsing and kept to myself." Aidan looked to the hills in the west where the sun hung low and painted the landscape in colours so rich it seemed possible to lick them of the hills like they were popsicles.

"You said there were witnesses. When I read the file, it said you were the only witness to what happened to Alex." Lane studied Aidan's eyes.

Her skin flushed red. "Look! How come when a First Nations deaf and gay kid gets killed, the case doesn't get solved? When two white guys die, then everyone wants answers?" Aidan looked at each of them in turn.

"Actually, it looks like four people besides Alex have died. We still have two of the five unaccounted for," Lane said.

"You have to do what you have to do. I told the RCMP everything I knew. It all happened so fast I couldn't be sure, but I knew who it was. I just couldn't prove it was Blake Rogers. He lied through his teeth, and the other three kept their mouths shut. Now it looks like they're all dead. What's the point in probing any deeper?"

Lane decided it was time to stop beating around the bush. "There's still a murderer out there. Is it you?"

Aidan shook her head. She looked directly at Lane. "I didn't, couldn't kill anyone. After I saw what Alex's murder did to Eva, I don't think I could ever kill anyone."

To Lane, it almost sounded like a regretful apology.

"Do you know where we can find Norm?" Lane waited for a change in her eyes.

"Nope." Aidan pushed herself off the tailgate.

She's lying, Lane thought.

"I'm going home to sleep, unless of course, you've got other questions."

"Where can we get in touch with you?" Harper asked.

"I live at Eva's." Aidan waited for Lane to get off the tailgate. She closed it, got in the cab and drove away.

Lane walked in the back door just after sundown. Twilight promised another half hour of summer light.

"The kids took the dog for a walk." Arthur sat at the kitchen table. His ears and neck were sunburned.

"The fight's over?" Lane went to the fridge for a glass of water.

"For now."

Lane looked over the water glass at Arthur.

Arthur's eyes held tired determination. "We need to talk."

Lane sat down.

"Erinn got the kids talking on the way home. They're afraid."

"Of what?" Lane asked.

Arthur gave him an *Are you completely blind?* expression. "You've been shot at twice, wounded once. Do I have to draw you pictures? They're worried about you. They've already lost their families, such as they were, and they're beginning to think this might be their family, although they didn't put it exactly like that. And there's more."

Lane took a deep breath, let it out slow. *This just gets more and more complicated,* he thought.

"Christine went to your brother first when she left Paradise. She stayed there for a day but couldn't stay any longer." Arthur turned on the kitchen light.

"Oh." *Being Christine's second choice hurts more than I thought it would.*

"It was obvious your niece wanted Christine there but her parents did not. We were her last stop before ..."

"Before what?" Lane asked.

"She didn't get specific, but she was headed out of

town. Who knows if we would have heard from her again?" Arthur rubbed the stubble on his chin. "The question is not how did we end up with two kids. It's how are we going to survive raising them?"

"And how do we all manage to stay together?"

"According to Erinn all we have to do is accept them." Arthur shook his head.

Lane laughed out loud. "There's irony for you!"

Arthur's shoulders sagged. "And they're not the only ones who are afraid of what's going to happen to you."

chapter 17

"Did you like the show?" Eva asked. They sat in her kitchen eating saskatoon muffins and drinking coffee.

Aidan sat across from Lane. There were dark circles under her eyes.

"I couldn't take my eyes off the puppets," Lane said.

Aidan frowned.

"What?" Lane asked.

"They're marionettes." Eva looked at Lane with a face free of judgement.

"Sorry. They seemed to come alive. One moment they were marionettes and the next they were real," Lane said.

"I'm sorry, I mean thank you. I hoped that would happen." Aidan's face went red.

"Was it like a documentary?" Lane buttered a muffin but kept his eyes on Aidan.

"Everything you saw, except of course for most of Alex's lines, happened." Aidan looked directly back at Lane.

"Alex loved to dance. We travelled around the country to powwows every summer," Eva said. "No one could dance like he could."

"Did you see the truck that hit him?" Lane looked at Eva.

"No." Eva shook her head.

"There was more than one witness, though." Lane made sure to fill his tone with confident certainty.

Eva looked at Aidan. Eva said, "He found out yesterday."

"You were there?" Lane asked.

"Of course. Saw you," Eva said.

"I didn't see you," Lane said.

"You were too busy watching the show. I left with the drummers." Eva looked at Aidan. "Was there someone else who saw what happened to Alex?"

Aidan looked at Eva. "Yes."

"Who?" Eva touched Aidan's hand.

Aidan stood up. She looked at Eva before turning and leaving the kitchen.

Eva looked at Lane and Harper in turn. Her face was a mask.

"We need to know," Harper said.

Eva said, "What good will that do?"

"There are two other families who don't know what happened to their sons." Lane cut his muffin and ate half.

"What will it cost?" Eva asked.

"I'm not sure what you mean?" Lane studied Eva's expression.

"The more you dig, the deeper you get, the more it costs. Is it time to stop digging?" Eva kept her eyes on Lane.

"We need to find out what happened to the two who haven't been found yet. Just like we needed to find out who was responsible for what happened to Alex." Lane brushed the crumbs from his fingers.

Eva shrugged. "Make sure the hole you dig isn't too deep to crawl out of."

Lane tried to smile but could not.

As they thanked Eva and made ready to leave, she said, "Norm took it hard. When his mom was dying, she gave him a job. Something to make him feel better. She asked Norm to look out for Alex. Norm never grew up enough to know that sometimes it's hard to keep a promise like that. Besides, Norm didn't know that I promised his mom I would look out for him."

Outside, Aidan's truck sat behind their Chev in the driveway.

Lane and Harper got into the Chev.

Lane said, "Norm's place?"

"That's the next step. Erinn has been on my case about making sure we have backup since the last two shootings. We'd better call it in," Harper said.

"Do you think we'll be overdoing it? You know, maybe scaring Norm?"

"You got shot. We don't want any more people getting shot." Harper pulled out onto the gravel road and turned left. He called in a request for assistance.

Lane thought about saying, "Let's leave him alone," but then changed his mind. That decision was to haunt him for the rest of his life.

Ten minutes later, their trailing cloud of dust drifted east as they eased into Norm's driveway and parked. "There's his machine." Harper pointed at the four-wheel ATV parked near the front door of Norm's freshly painted white wartime house with one bedroom above and kitchen and sitting room below. Along the southern line of the property was a wall of wood being dried for winter. On the northern side there were two sheds in front of a line of mature pine trees. Next to the trees, an ancient yellow road grader sat rusting in grass reaching as high as its tires. A crop of potatoes grew knee-deep from the house to the driveway.

There was the sound of a truck approaching. It downshifted and Aidan drove up behind them.

Harper said, "I'll keep an eye out."

Lane got out of the car and walked back to Aidan.

"You'll scare him. Let me talk with him." Aidan made to open the door of her truck.

Lane held her door shut. "When did you know that Norm was the other person who saw what happened when Alex was run down?"

Aidan kept her eyes on the house. "A couple of days ago. He didn't tell us when it happened, because he couldn't get the words out. And, he didn't think anyone would believe him. You have to understand, he's just a kid!"

"Aidan, you okay?" The voice came from an open window on the first floor of Norm's house.

"Norm?" Aidan said.

"Yep."

Lane tried to spot Norm through the window but could not.

"I'm fine, Norm!" Aidan said to Lane, "Let me go to him."

"Will you stand with me behind the truck?" Lane asked.

"Okay."

Lane said, "Norm?"

"Yep!"

"Is it okay if Aidan and I move to the back of the truck?" Lane thought he might be making a mistake but thought, *You're committed now.*

"Sure! That other fella want to go there too?" Norm asked.

"Yes!" Harper said.

"Go ahead!" Norm said.

Lane kept his eyes on the window as the three of them moved to the back of the pickup. He feared seeing a muzzle flash before they could crouch behind the truck.

"Feel better?" Norm asked.

"Yes!" Lane said.

"Aidan? Is Eva okay?" Norm asked.

"She's fine!" Aidan looked from Lane to Harper and kept her voice low when she said, "He won't hurt anyone."

"Sorry I shot you in the hind quarters! I thought you two was takin' Eva away to jail that day! My mother told me to watch out for Eva. Eva's like a mother to me. She's done nothin' wrong!" Norm said.

Lane heard the approach of a helicopter. He thought, *Pretty soon, he won't be able to hear me.* "Apology accepted! Can you come on out now?"

"I waited a year for those guys to get arrested before I gave that first one a lead pill in the ear! I think I'll wait a while longer! Is that the police helicopter?" Norm asked.

"I think so!" Lane thought, *Go for it.* "Thanks for saving our lives at Blake's place! We didn't have a chance up against that rifle of his!"

"I rode over there after Blake said those things to Eva at the Super Service. I saw him firin' his gun and walkin' toward your car! Someone had to do something, or he woulda killt ya both!"

The helicopter was close now. Its rotor made conversation impossible.

They looked up. The police machine made a slow pass.

They've seen us huddled here. They'll be setting up roadblocks and alerting the tactical team next, Lane thought.

The helicopter flew north.

Lane looked at Aidan. He said, "Norm, it's going to get very crowded around here very soon. Please come out now!"

"Tell 'em to stay out of the potato patch. Them potatoes is for Eva and Aidan!"

Aidan said, "Norm! Come out, Norm!"

Lane pulled out his cell and turned to Aidan. "What's his phone number?"

"He doesn't have a phone," Aidan said.

The helicopter made another pass. It made a sharp

turn over Norm's house. Lane could see the pilot looking down on them. Lane waved. The pilot nodded once.

Harper's cellphone rang. "Harper."

Aidan started to move out of cover.

Lane grabbed her arm.

"He won't hurt me." She struggled to free herself from Lane.

Lane pulled out a pair of handcuffs. "I'll cuff you to the bumper if you move again."

"Shithead!" Aidan sat on the bumper.

Harper spoke into his phone. "The suspect has made no threatening moves. He's admitted to shooting Blake Rogers and apologized for shooting Detective Lane. He also made a direct reference to at least one of the disappearances. Norm's only request has been that we stay out of his potato patch." Harper listened, looked at Aidan and then at Lane. Harper closed his phone. "We sit tight."

They waited in silence for the first few minutes as the helicopter circled nearby.

"Blake and his friends were gay, right?" Aidan looked at Lane.

"It looks that way." Lane kept his eyes on Norm's house.

"You're gay, right?" Aidan asked.

Lane looked at her.

"Eva told me." Aidan looked right back at Lane.

"Yes, I am." *Where is this going?* Lane thought.

"How come Blake was always acting so macho, then? I mean it doesn't make sense. He was gay. So what? Why did he have to be so damned cruel?" Aidan asked.

Lane shrugged. "People are people. Some are like you, me, Harper, Eva, and some aren't. Assuming that Blake will be a certain type of person because he's gay is just that, an assumption."

Harper said, "They're here."

The first of the black-outfitted tactical team appeared behind the shed. Another took up a position on this side of the woodpile.

The helicopter hovered just far enough away so that conversation was possible.

Before Lane could speak, an unfamiliar voice came from the trees along the north side of the property. "Norm?"

"Who are you?" Norm asked.

"Smith. John Smith."

Lane studied the trees but couldn't see the officer.

The silence lasted thirty seconds.

"Shit!" Harper pointed to Lane's left.

A black-clad officer with an automatic rifle crawled past them and wiggled down the middle of the potato patch.

Harper dialled and spoke into his phone. "What's the guy doing in the potatoes?"

"Norm? Go out the door facing the woodpile. Keep your hands in the air!" Smith said.

"He'll get confused! He gets confused when there are too many people around!" Aidan said. "How many times do I have to explain that he's just a kid?"

Lane looked at her. There were tears in her eyes.

"Look!" Harper pointed.

Norm stood in the yard. He was wearing his cowboy hat with the string tied under the chin. His gun belt was slung low around his hips. There was no pistol in the holster. Norm held a rifle above his head like he was acting out a scene from a movie.

Lane had a flash of memory. He remembered the bolt action and box of shells in Eva's kitchen cupboard. He went to shout a warning, thought better of it and turned to Harper. "That rifle is a twenty-two?"

"Looks like it." Harper looked hard at Lane. "No bolt action, right?"

"And no shells," Lane said.

"What's happening?" Aidan asked.

"Put the rifle down!" Smith spoke as the officer in the potato patch stood up with his weapon trained on Norm.

Norm turned and dropped his arms. The rifle was across his chest and pointed in the general direction of the tactical officer in the potatoes.

"Norm's rifle is useless!" Lane stepped out from behind the pickup.

Someone said, "Put the fucking weapon down!"

"There are no bullets in the suspect's weapon!" Lane said.

Norm looked around, spotting another tactical team member.

Lane stood in the open with his arms waving.

Norm turned in Lane's direction. "Those potatoes are for Eva."

Three shots were fired in rapid succession.

Lane stood horrified as two holes appeared in Norm's chest. Another caught him in the throat. Blood poured down along his shoulder, to his elbow and onto the ground.

Norm looked at his chest and the blood. He dropped the rifle and clutched at his wounds. He spat blood. It spilled over his chin. He sat down.

"Norm!" Aidan said. "Let me go, you bastard!"

Lane looked to his right. Aidan's legs kicked straight out as Harper held her by the waist.

When Lane looked at Norm, there was a black form leaning over the fallen man with his hand at Norm's neck. The officer spoke into his radio. He looked at the officer in the potato patch and shook his head.

Two men went inside the house and returned. "Clear!"

The officer who'd fired the shots took his helmet and balaclava off. He turned to face Lane.

"Stockwell," Lane said.

Stockwell smiled. He moved his left index finger in the air as if he were putting the number one on a scoreboard.

"You fucking idiot!" Aidan's voice was distorted with rage and grief.

Lane turned.

Harper had Aidan by the waist. Her feet were running but not touching the ground. Her face was wild with rage.

It took both of them to hold her back.

"You fucking murderer!" Aidan screamed at Stockwell.

The officer near the body said, "His gun's empty. It's useless. No way it could fire!"

Aidan began to weep. Lane looked at the still form of Norm on the grass. Paramedics ran past. They made their way to Norm and began to attempt to revive him.

Harper started to say something, decided not to, and shook his head.

Later, when Lane could talk with them, the officers on the roadblock said Eva walked past, ignoring their commands. She just looked at them when they went to stop her. "There was just no way I was going to cuff that old woman and drag her into the back seat of the unit," one officer explained.

Eva's eyes met Lane's as she approached. Harper stood to one side. Eva looked at Norm's body then put her arms around Aidan. Harper stared at Norm's body.

"He got confused. You know how he watches old movies? He came out with the rifle held above his head just like in a movie. He didn't want anyone in his potato patch. The potatoes were for us!" The words spilled out of Aidan. "How could this happen? Wasn't Alex enough?"

Eva looked past Aidan toward Norm. She looked at Lane and Harper. "Who shot him?" she asked.

Both detectives looked over at Stockwell, who stood in the potatoes, speaking with another officer who stood just inside the patch.

Eva turned to Aidan, "Wait here."

Lane followed as Eva walked toward Stockwell. When she got within a few metres of him, Stockwell turned.

"What's *she* doing here?" Stockwell asked.

Lane heard the arrogance in Stockwell's voice. Eva took the scene in without a word. Lane saw the name McTavish on the other officer's black outfit.

"Get out of the garden." Eva stood a good head shorter than Stockwell.

McTavish had his grey hair cut short. He looked directly at Lane who looked directly back at him.

"What did you say?" Stockwell sounded as if he couldn't believe what he was hearing.

"Norm." Eva nodded in the direction of Norm's body and the paramedics administering CPR. "He didn't like people walking in his potatoes. Respect his memory."

"What the fuck is she talking about?" Stockwell smiled at McTavish.

Lane kept his eyes on McTavish. He stared back at Lane with grey cold eyes. McTavish looked at Eva.

"It's about respect," Lane said.

"What kind of politically correct bullshit is this?" Stockwell crossed his arms as if the decision were already made.

Mctavish looked down and carefully moved one foot to the empty space between the hilled potatoes. In a few steps, he was out of the crop without doing any further damage.

The three of them stood at the edge of the potatoes, looking at Stockwell. Lane looked around him, the eyes of each officer in the yard focused on Stockwell.

"I'm not fucking moving because she says so!" Stockwell said.

McTavish kept silent, but his eyes were on Stockwell.

Lane looked at Eva. He saw in her eyes that she might easily step forward and cut Stockwell's throat.

Lane could feel the rage rising off of her. He thought, *Go ahead Eva, I won't stop you.*

Stockwell walked straight out of the patch, each step deliberately crushing a plant where its stalk met the soil.

Lane watched Eva. She kept her eyes on Stockwell.

He turned his back on her and marched away.

Lane looked around. The other officers watched Stockwell with undisguised contempt.

Eva looked at Lane and then McTavish. She said, "Norm was a child in his heart. Treat his body like you would treat a child's?"

"Of course," McTavish said.

She looked at the paramedics. "It's over. His spirit's gone."

Lane nodded.

"We will be at my place if you need us." Eva walked back to Aidan. Aidan got in the passenger side of her pickup. Harper opened the door so Eva could climb in behind the wheel. She started the engine and waited for other vehicles to get out of the way before reversing and driving away.

McTavish looked at Lane. "I saw you stepping away from cover. Why?"

"I realized Norm's weapon was useless. I was too late." Lane felt as if he were in a hole and someone was shoveling guilt down on him.

"Norm shot the cowboy who was shooting at you?" McTavish asked.

"Yes," Lane said.

"And the others?" McTavish asked.

"Norm killed two of the men who were in the truck that ran down Eva's grandson." Lane felt Harper's hand at his back.

McTavish turned to Harper. "The bodies of the two who are missing?"

"Yes, we don't know where they are for certain," Harper said.

McTavish said, "You know, after the facts about this shooting get out, there'll be hell to pay. Stockwell was acting like a cowboy."

After several more hours at the scene, Harper drove them back to the city. When they passed the Super Service gas station, he said, "What do we do now?"

Lane made no attempt to hide his anger when he said, "We have to find the missing men! This whole mess needs to be cleared up and out in the open before it will be finished!"

TUESDAY, JULY 16

chapter 18

"We're not walking on egg shells in this house for one more second!" Arthur said.

Lane had just yelled at Roz, who'd touched his hand with a cold nose. He watched as she ducked away, then returned with her tail wagging to say all was forgiven. It was then that Lane remembered Roz begging forgiveness from the woman who'd found the body of Skip Lombardi along the Elbow River. The woman who drove away with the abandoned Roz running behind. He thought, *Shit! By the time I remember anything it's too late!*

"What?" Arthur looked across the cold cuts, potato salad, and pickles set out for dinner. Matt and Christine were looking for an exit. Arthur looked at each of them and said, "You two stay put. I'm tired of walking on eggshells with the two of you as well!"

Lane looked at Roz. He offered his open hand. She came to get her neck rubbed. "I took too long to put evidence together, and a man died because of it."

"You shot him?" Arthur glared at Lane across the table.

Lane felt the intensity of the look and felt his skin flush. "No. But if I'd put it together a minute earlier, I could have stopped someone else from shooting him."

Arthur's voice oozed sarcasm when he said, "So not only are you responsible for your actions, now you're responsible for the actions of others! Give me a break. I'm sorry to tell you this, but the entire world doesn't revolve around you."

Anger flashed in Lane. "The poor bastard was only a kid!"

"And he was over fifty!" Arthur reached for a slice of garlic beef. "Let's not forget that fact! In fact let's not forget who shot him. An officer who likes crowd control duty so he can bash a few heads."

Lane looked sideways at Arthur.

Arthur said, "You know I listen to your conversations. I know what cops talk about!"

Christine and Matt kept their hands at their sides.

Lane glared at Arthur.

Arthur picked up the plate of pickled beets. "It happened. It shouldn't have, but it happened. Sometimes that's all there is to be learned."

Lane shook his head. He reached for his napkin. Roz poked his elbow with her nose.

Arthur said, "And let's not forget that you were wounded. All four of us are still dealing with that. Harper is taking a couple of days off. Erinn's a wreck after this latest shooting. Now," he turned to Christine and Matt, "what's been eating you two? We're going to begin talking about what's bothering everyone instead of fighting. I'm a nervous eater." He grabbed the bowl of potato salad and began scooping it onto his plate. "If things don't start to calm down around here, I'll gain twenty kilos!"

"You want me to leave, don't you?" Christine started to stand.

"Who said anything about that?" Arthur started putting potato salad on Christine's plate until she sat back down. "We're solving a problem." He held the spoon erect. "Maybe other families aren't like this, but this is how this family solves its problems. We talk!" He flicked the spoon for effect. A dollop of potato salad flew across the table.

Lane wiped potato salad from his face.

Matt covered his mouth.

Arthur began scooping more potato salad onto his plate. "It's not fair if the three of you can get angry, and I gain all the weight!"

Matt pointed at the potato salad. "And it's not fair if the rest of us starve because you won't share."

Arthur looked at the bowl. He'd scooped it clean of all the salad. The mound on Arthur's plate covered the beets and meat he'd already piled there.

Matt's eyes got wide as he realized what he'd said could ignite a bigger argument.

Arthur began to laugh.

Within a breath, they all joined in, including the dog, who howled at Lane's side. Lane looked at Roz and then at the people around the table. He thought, *We've all been abandoned, just like Aidan and Alex. Maybe that's why we fight like hell to stay together.*

The laughter faded.

Lane said, "I just realized I met Roz before we adopted her."

"Tell us," Matt said.

Lane began to laugh. "Maybe after supper."

The first question Matt asked after dinner was, "Where did you meet Roz before?"

"I don't know. It might make you think less of her," Lane said.

"We're not stupid," Christine said.

"I know …" Lane began.

"Then let us decide for ourselves," Matt said.

Arthur smiled, then took another sip of wine.

"When we went to see the body of the man by the river, Roz was there. She tried to pull the body out of the water. Roz's owner thought Roz was eating the corpse. The forensic examiner on the scene could find no evidence that Roz did anything but try to pull the man away from the water. The woman who owned her was upset and abandoned Roz in the parking lot." Lane looked at Roz, who lay on her belly in the middle of the front-room floor. Her head was cocked to one side as she tried to follow the conversation.

"So that's how she ended up on Glenmore Trail?" Christine asked.

Lane nodded. "Apparently, Roz ran until the pads

on her paws were worn down. She sat down on the road and caused a traffic jam."

"That's bullshit! She does nothing wrong and gets abandoned!"

Matt said.

Lane thought, *Matt's angrier than he needs to be.* Then he realized, *Maybe he's got every right to be angry.*

"The question is, how do you feel about her now?" Arthur asked.

"Lucky us," Christine said. "We ended up with Roz."

And, Lane thought, *lucky us, we ended up with the three of you.*

Harper stood in the middle of the kitchen, wincing each time a cupboard door slammed.

Erinn worked her way from cupboard to cupboard, starting with the one located next to the fridge, then around to the stove. She opened each door and slammed it.

Harper heard the screams of his daughter coming from her bedroom.

"Who lives like this?!" Erinn slammed another cupboard door. Something ceramic tumbled inside.

"Erinn," Harper said.

"I can't live like this! The baby! Glenn! What do we do when you don't come home?!" Erinn finished at the stove and walked across the kitchen to the fridge, ready to begin the slamming all over again.

Harper reached for her arm.

She pulled away. Her face was red with rage, her eyes wild from fear and lack of sleep.

"What's going on?" Glenn leaned in the doorway leading downstairs. He crossed his arms and looked around the kitchen. His gaze stopped at Erinn, who was catching her breath, her wild eyes locked on him.

"I can see why you're tired of this kitchen, I mean, it matches the walls. Pretty beige if you ask me. If you want, we can go look at some colours." Glenn leaned his head to the right and focused on his uncle.

Harper moved to Erinn and put his arms around her. Erinn struggled, then began to weep.

"I'll go get Jessica," Glenn said.

Lane's mind was somewhere between asleep and awake when the phone rang.

Arthur answered it, "Hello? Harper? Just a minute." He handed the phone to Lane.

Lane took the phone, "What's up?"

Harper said, "I'm going to take a few more days off. Erinn finally fell asleep. She was freaking out."

Lane's mind filled with a myriad of questions. "You okay?"

"I hope so." Harper hung up.

"What's the matter?" Arthur took the phone as Lane handed it to him.

"Erinn's freaking out." Lane looked at the ceiling of their bedroom.

"I don't blame her." Arthur rolled onto his shoulder with his back to Lane.

The phone rang again five hours later.

Arthur tried to pick up the phone and dropped it on the rug. He reached for the fallen phone then fell after it. "Hello?"

"For you." Arthur handed the phone to Lane.

Lane's shoulder and chest muscles complained from the aftereffects of the exploding air bag as he reached for the phone. "Hello."

"Detective Lane?" the chief asked.

Lane eased his feet out of bed and sat up. He winced at the pain from his wound. "Yes."

"A barricade has been set up across the highway near the edge of the city limits, not far from the scene of the most recent shooting. You know the location?" The chief's voice sounded tired.

"Yes." Lane looked at the clock on the night table. It was fifteen minutes after four.

"A woman named Eva Starchild has asked for you specifically. She needs you at the barricade by five A M. Detective Harper is unavailable?"

"That's correct." Lane stood up. He heard Arthur climbing back into bed.

"A cruiser is en route to you. It will take you to the scene. The driver will be there within the next five minutes. The officer escorting you has been ordered to keep me apprised of the situation. Take your phone." The chief hung up.

Lane reached for his clothes.

When he made it downstairs, red and blue lights reached inside, illuminating the way. He stepped into his shoes, grabbed a jacket, stepped outside, and locked the door.

Lane walked to the cruiser. The outside air was fresh and cool on his face. He leaned down and looked inside the car. The driver waved at him. He had the seat all the way back, but was still crammed in behind the wheel. Lane got in. The driver's hand dwarfed Lane's when they shook hands. Lane spotted a black braid of hair as the driver shoulder checked.

"Oscar," the officer said as Lane buckled up.

"Lane."

Oscar kept the lights on but didn't use the siren. Lane saw almost no traffic as Oscar raced down into the river valley.

"The barricade is set up within city limits. The chief is trying to keep it quiet and wants a low profile for as long as possible. She thinks the best way to find a solution is without the glare of cameras." Oscar drove over the bridge.

Lane looked at the cruiser's lights reflected over the Bow River. "How many on the barricades?" He opened his window to let in some air. *My mind's got to be sharp for this!*

"The estimate is ten to fifteen." Oscar braked for a four-way stop. He looked from left to right.

Lane was pushed back as Oscar touched the accelerator. "Armed?"

Oscar nodded. "The spotter says mostly hunting rifles and shotguns." Oscar used his thumb to point at the back seat. "There's a Glock and a holster for you."

They began their climb out of the river valley. On the left, the lights of downtown lit up the belly of a black sky.

Oscar opened up the engine along Sarcee Trail. They roared up the hill.

"You're liking this," Lane said.

Oscar grinned. "You bet."

"Anything more I need to know?" Lane asked.

"As soon as you've checked out the situation, the chief wants you to call her. Got your phone?"

Lane pulled it out of his jacket pocket. The air rushed in the window, buffeting him. He shivered and closed the window. "Anywhere we can stop for some coffee?" He thought, *There's just no way I'm going to watch anyone else get shot.*

In ten minutes they approached the police roadblock and were waved through. Lane balanced two trays of coffees on his knees.

"I'm trying not to spill any." Oscar dodged a rough spot in the road.

They cruised past the Super Service gas bar. Lane saw that it was closed. Four police cruisers and a van were parked under the lights. Officers gathered around a map they had spread across the hood of one of the cruisers.

Up ahead, a flashlight waved at them. Two blue and white cruisers were parked across the highway. Oscar stopped for the officer with the flashlight.

The officer leaned to see inside the cruiser. "Who are you?" he said to Lane.

"Lane. You want us to walk from here?" Lane asked.

The officer nodded. He pointed at the side of the highway. "Park over there."

Oscar parked on the shoulder. He took a tray of coffees from Lane. "Don't forget the Glock."

Lane eased out with the coffees and set his tray on the hood of the car, then opened the back door, reached for the Glock, and put it on. Oscar went to talk with the officers at the cruisers, then returned.

"They're set up about fifty metres down the road. I checked with the spotters. The people on the barricade are quiet. Probably waiting for sunrise." Oscar looked over his shoulder at the horizon, where there was a hint of purple.

Lane took one tray of coffees from Oscar and picked up the other from the hood. "Any sign of Eva?"

Oscar shook his head. "Not yet." He went to say more and closed his mouth.

Lane walked along the highway toward the next pair of police cars. Oscar followed.

"She's my auntie. Watch out for her, will you?" Oscar looked toward the barricade.

Lane nodded. He looked at his watch and saw that it was five o'clock.

The officers at the cruisers watched the two men approach. One officer said, "The tactical unit is on its way. We're to sit tight and wait for them."

"What's that coming this way?" Lane looked south, where three sets of headlights travelled west, parallel to the highway they stood on. Oscar and the other officers turned to watch.

Lane stepped between the grills of the cruisers blocking the highway. He followed the yellow line as the darkness deepened. He looked up. No stars or planets winked back. The darkness became so complete that he relied on his feet and ears while waiting for his eyes to adjust.

"Lane?" Oscar asked.

Lane kept walking.

Ahead, he saw the straight lines and angles of a silhouette gradually becoming a road grader parked across the highway. In front of the grader was a mound. Lane stopped. "Eva?"

Silence.

There, as the whisper of a twig scratching up against fabric on his right. Fear grabbed for his belly. He swallowed. *What was I thinking, standing out here with eight cups of coffee in the middle of an armed stand-off?* "Eva?"

"She's not here." The matter-of-fact voice came from behind the barricade.

Hooves clattered across the pavement. Something brushed across his back and disappeared into the ditch on the left.

"What was that?" Lane's heart raced and his legs shook. He forced himself to breathe.

Another voice to his right said, "Just a deer. You startled it."

Lane tried to slow his breathing.

The sound of engines made Lane look to his left. Three pairs of headlights bounced across an open field.

Lane could sense the tension rising around him. He stood there, holding the coffee and wishing there was a bathroom nearby.

The lights came closer. The sound of their engines made it impossible for Lane to hear what the men were doing at the barricade. *Whoever is hidden on my right probably has me in his sights,* Lane thought.

Lane could see that two of the approaching vehicles were pickup trucks and the third, with its close-set headlights, was a tractor.

The pickups stopped at the far side of the fence. Two

people climbed out of the back of one truck; a third got out of the cab and walked toward the fence.

"Hang on fellas, it's just us! We brought food." It was a woman's voice.

Two of the women put their feet on the bottom strands of barbed wire and lifted the top wire with their hands. The third woman grunted as she bent down to step under the wire. As she stood, she turned and held the wire for the other two.

"Hang on fellas! It's me, Eva!" She walked down into the ditch, tripped, and fell to her knees.

Lane put the coffees down on the yellow line and moved to help her. She was up before he could get there.

"You okay, Eva?" another woman asked.

"Fine! Get that fence down for the backhoe!"

The women at the wire each moved to a fence post.

Lane could hear the wire complain as the women used pliers to pull rusty nails away from the wood.

Lane felt the wet of the dew at his ankles. He offered Eva his hand. She grabbed his elbow. They climbed out of the ditch.

They stepped onto the pavement.

Lane picked up the coffees. "Want a coffee?"

Eva looked in his direction. In the growing light it was possible to see the features of her face. She wore a heavy coat, a ball cap, and a smile. "'Bout time *you* brought *me* coffee."

Lane held the tray. She took a cup and pulled at the plastic cover. "Got more?" she whispered.

Lane nodded.

"You boys want some coffee?" Eva asked.

Silence was her answer.

"Bruce, Elliott, Everett? I know you're there. Your mother told me you three helped move Norm's grader last night. You come on out and get a coffee! You must be cold. It'll warm you up! Your mom is in the truck on the other side of the fence." Eva lifted her coffee in greeting.

A man appeared from behind an evergreen in the ditch. Another materialized from the opposite side of the road, next to one of the women working at the fence.

Two more crawled out of the trench cut across the pavement.

Lane handed out coffees. The men cradled their weapons as they formed a circle around Eva. "Two more coffees left!" Eva said.

Another man stepped out from behind the ancient grader. He hopped over the trench. When he reached them, Eva handed him a cup.

They stood there in silence, sipping their coffees.

The engine of the backhoe belched a cloud of diesel smoke. It inched nearer to the fence. The women at the fence posts had the wire down on the ground, keeping it there with their feet as the backhoe hobbled over the uneven ground, nosed down into the ditch, then crawled up the other side and onto the pavement. The cab lights revealed a driver wearing a pink ball cap and red satin jacket.

Eva waved at the driver. "Judith! Shut it down."

The clatter of the diesel died.

In the fresh quiet, Eva said, "We're gonna have

breakfast. Then we're gonna talk. Your mothers and aunties are in the trucks. We've been talkin'. We don't want anyone else to die. Lost Norm and Alex and four other boys. That's enough." Eva pointed her coffee at Lane. "The policeman's here 'cause I invited him. He's the one got shot by Norm."

Eva waved at the pickup trucks. The engines started up and the trucks moved forward. Dipping and bouncing, they eased their way in and out of the ditch, then parked between the protesters and the police.

The woman driving one pickup opened the door and looked into the crowd. She nodded at one of the men who nodded back. Similar greetings occurred within the group of women and men.

Within five minutes the women had coolers out and more coffee. The coolers held sandwiches, muffins, bread, fried potatoes, and bacon. Paper plates were distributed. People stood alone or in groups, talking quietly while eating and sipping from coffees resting on hoods and tailgates.

Eva looked at Lane. "Come on. Get something to eat."

Lane's phone began to vibrate. He pulled it out of his pocket. "Lane."

"McTavish here. We've just arrived. We're wondering if you need some assistance."

Lane looked at the faces of the men and women around him. "We're just having breakfast."

"What?" McTavish said.

"Who's with you?" Lane asked.

"Don't worry, Stockwell is not on this detail. He's

off duty until the shooting has been investigated." McTavish sounded insulted that Lane had even asked the question.

"At this stage, everything is fine. Give us some space. Eva's looking for a solution and it'll take time." Lane looked east. The sun was painting the horizon red and orange. A layer of solid cloud left a gap so the sun could paint the belly of the overcast.

"Check in with me every fifteen minutes or I'll be calling you. The chief is pretty specific about that. She doesn't want anyone else hurt." McTavish was blunt to the point of being rude.

"None of us want that." Lane looked at the sky as the top half of the sun rose, ripe and orange. He looked at the people, could see their faces now, their teeth when one or two smiled. A mother hugged a son. A wife touched a husband's hand. Eva watched it all.

Lane thought, *There are more officers at the road-blocks, policemen putting on their body armour and checking their weapons, and scouts watching us through night vision goggles.* Someone touched his elbow. He looked to his right. Aidan offered him a sandwich.

"Egg salad. My specialty." She sipped at her coffee and watched him over the rim of the cup.

"Thanks." Lane unwrapped the sandwich. It was thick whole-wheat bread. There were sweet pickles in the mix with the egg. Lane was ravenous. "This tastes wonderful. I haven't had breakfast yet."

"So, it tastes wonderful only because you haven't eaten?" Aidan asked.

Lane could swear Aidan was smiling behind the coffee cup.

"You're enjoying this." Lane waved his sandwich in the general direction of the barricade.

She nodded. "I like to see people stick up for themselves."

Lane looked at the rifles and shotguns leaning up against the trucks. "I'd prefer it was done without weapons."

She pointed at his Glock. "So would I."

"Fair enough. How come you're talking to me today?" Lane asked.

"Eva likes you. She doesn't like everybody. And I saw you try to save Norm. You didn't try to stop Eva from cutting Stockwell down to size after the bastard killed Norm." Her voice choked at the mention of Norm's name. "And you stopped me from running into the middle of the whole mess."

"I regret not thinking quickly enough to save Norm." Lane looked at his coffee and sandwich.

"That's my big regret about Alex. But Alex is dead and so is Norm." Aidan shrugged.

Lane looked around. "Maybe that's why Eva is here. One less regret."

Aidan said, "It's time to talk. At least that's what Eva says. When she talks, people tend to listen. And most of these people have been at her sweat. They'll listen to her if they'll listen to anyone."

Eva looked toward the barricade. "Any more fellas there?"

"Just me," a voice said.

"Come on out. Time to talk," Eva said.

A man stepped out from behind the barricade. He carried a rifle with a scope mounted on top. Lane saw that it was Al from the gas station.

"Come on over, Al," Eva said.

A woman, who Lane assumed was Al's wife, said, "Coffee's good." She handed Al a cup when he got close enough.

Lane saw the golden eagle amulet at Al's throat, his buckskin jacket, pants, and moccasins. Over top of it all he wore a black waterproof canvas coat reaching to his heels. The coat matched the colour of his stetson. Lane looked around, studying the reactions of the First Nations people to Al's European attempt at transforming himself into an aboriginal. Most faces revealed neither distaste nor acceptance. Only one young man smiled and shook his head at Al's outfit.

Eva handed Al a sandwich and the last cup of coffee Lane had brought with him.

The sun was high enough now to hide itself behind the solid cloud cover. Their part of this world was half-lit somewhere between sunrise and sunset.

"We've got some time," Eva said. "How much?" Eva looked at Lane. All eyes turned in his direction.

"How much do you need?" Lane asked.

"Hard to say," Eva said.

Lane pulled out his phone, recalled the chief's number, pressed a button, and waited.

"Lane?" the chief asked.

"We need some time. Eva's got everyone together to talk," Lane said.

"Do you trust Eva?" the chief asked.

Lane nodded. "Yes."

"How much time do you need?"

"I'm not sure." Lane waited.

The chief took some time to reply. "I'll get you as much time as I can. Pretty soon someone from the province will be calling me and then someone from Ottawa. The media will get wind of this if they haven't already. It'll be a circus in no time. Who knows how much time you'll have? I'll get in touch with McTavish for you. You call him in two minutes. Keep him in the loop?"

"Okay. Thanks." Lane closed his phone and looked at Eva. "The chief of police is giving us as much time as possible. I'm not sure how much."

Eva nodded. "Let's get started."

Lane called McTavish. "Sit tight. We're trying to sort this thing out."

McTavish said, "Understood."

Lane closed his phone while nodding at Eva.

Eva sat on a tailgate at the edge of a rough circle where some leaned against the trucks, sat in lawn chairs, or stood together in pairs. She listened. The conversation flowed and ebbed as the people spoke of their issues. Some talked of the two years it took to find Alex's killers. Many wondered why Norm was killed. They asked if it were true that there were no bullets in his twenty-two rifle. Others talked of the city trying to push them off their land.

Lane watched Eva handle each issue with a nod or the one comment she repeated over and over again, "Six dead is enough."

Every fifteen minutes, Lane called McTavish with an update. If Lane forgot, someone in the circle would remind him.

Three or four hours later one woman said, "What about the guns?"

Her son stood, lifted his shot gun, ejected the shells, and set the weapon down in the middle of the highway. The women looked at each man in turn. In silence they waited as one man after another emptied his weapon and set it down next to a growing stockpile. An hour later, the group watched Al as he cradled his weapon in his arms, refusing to meet any of the eyes aimed at him.

Lane looked at their faces until he saw Aidan watching him. He thought, *Of course!*

He took his pistol out of its holster, ejected the clip, checked for a round in the barrel, then dismantled the Glock and set the pieces down next to the other weapons. He dropped the clip into his pocket, then stepped back to join the circle.

For thirty minutes they waited in silence until Al stood, took the scope off his rifle and slipped it into his pocket. He emptied the rifle and put it with the rest.

Eva said, "We're here today. We'll be here tomorrow. The city will not be able to take away T'suu T'ina lands if we stick together. The city is coming this way. We have no choice but to find a way to live with each other."

One of the men said, "We need to fill the hole in the road."

Judith walked to the backhoe, "I'll get it started."

One woman joked, "Judith was the one who dug it!"

Men and women grabbed shovels. Within half an hour, the trench was filled and tamped. They used the winch on one of the trucks to tow the grader off the road while the backhoe's bucket pushed the museum piece from behind. The grader was maneuvered through the ditch to the south side of the fence. Pretty soon, Lane was the only one on this side of the wire.

He stood in the middle of the highway next to the weapons. The barbed wire was tacked back onto the posts. Lane watched as the men and women packed into the pickups and backhoe.

He took his phone out of his pocket and dialled.

"Lane?" the chief asked.

"The road is repaired. The barrier is down. The weapons have been left in the middle of the highway. Please let McTavish know that the protesters are leaving and will be allowed to pass through road blocks without any interference. Without Eva, you know this probably wouldn't have ended peacefully. We got away with a warning." Lane closed his phone.

Eva watched him from the cab of a pickup truck where she sat with four women.

Lane's phone rang a minute later. He opened it.

"Lane?" McTavish asked.

"It's me. The protesters have disarmed themselves and will be allowed to go home without any delays. The weapons are here. Come get me and the weapons." Lane closed his phone after noting that it was after ten o'clock.

A police van pulled up within a minute. McTavish stepped out. He was dressed in his black tactical uniform. Without a word, he and Lane loaded the weapons into the back of the van.

As they drove back through the police barriers, McTavish nodded in the direction of the cameras set up on the gas station's lot. "Our deputy chief sure knows how to find the spotlight."

Lane turned to watch Deputy Chief Calvin Smoke smiling at the cameras and pointing at his chest.

chapter 19

Lane sat at the table on the deck, just off their kitchen. He sipped Arabica and watched Roz with her nose nestled between paws. The sun reflected off the neighbour's vinyl siding. He sat under an umbrella to protect him from nearly thirty degrees of heat.

The phone rang. He picked it up.

"Lane?" Harper asked.

"You okay? How about Erinn?" Lane asked.

"They're both sleeping. When Erinn found out about the last shooting, it was just too much. She started thinking about the time I was shot. She had a meltdown. Glenn and I have been busy taking care of her and Jessica. It's not easy because the baby is being breastfed. Erinn's finally getting some sleep instead of staying in bed and staring at the ceiling." Harper kept his voice at a whisper.

"How about you?" Lane looked at Roz. Her tail swept the deck.

"I'm hangin' in there. If it wasn't for Glenn, I don't know what I'd do. The kid's been cooking meals, helpin' with clean up, walking the baby, doing loads of wash. He's sleeping too."

"What's up?" Lane asked.

"I've been thinking about what you said about this case. About how it's not over until we find the two missing guys." Harper gave Lane a second to get up to speed.

"Have you been sleeping?" Lane asked.

"A couple of hours. My mind is on overdrive."

Lane asked, "Nightmares?"

"No. Nothing like that. It's the case. I can't stop thinking about it. Look at what's happened, all because it wasn't solved the first time around. We've got to find those two missing guys."

Lane felt Roz nudge his free hand. He began to rub her under the chin. "We have to go back to Eva's. The problem is that, after what's happened, I wouldn't blame her if she refused to allow us on her place. And there's the problem of where to start looking."

Harper thought for a minute. "I've been doing some research. There may be a likely search area."

"What have you been researching?" Lane asked.

Harper told him.

THURSDAY, JULY 18

ch*a*pter 20

"Christine got a job," Arthur sat at the table on the deck. He wore his housecoat to cut the chill of the early morning air.

"Where?" Lane stretched his legs out and sipped from his coffee. He thought, *What am I going to say to Eva when I get to her place?*

"The coffee shop. You know, the one Kuldeep runs." Arthur adjusted his housecoat.

"When was this?"

"Yesterday. She starts today," Arthur said.

"She seems in a rush to get on with her life," Lane said.

"And if she's living here for a while, we've got to make plans." Arthur leaned forward.

"Plans?"

"Christine will need to go to school in the fall," Arthur said.

Lane parked to one side of the burn mark in Eva's yard. Aidan's pickup truck was parked close to the Quonset. The inside back door of the house was open. The glass on the screen door sparkled.

Alone, Lane, turned off the engine, got out of the Chev, and listened to his feet crunch over gravel as he walked to the back door and knocked. He studied the fuchsia plant hanging next to the door.

Aidan came to the door. She smiled at him.

"Who is it?" Eva asked.

"Lane." Aidan crossed her arms.

Eva came to the door. Her hair was braided. She wore a sweatshirt and sweatpants. She looked at Lane. "Want a cup of coffee?"

"I'm coffeed out. How about a walk instead?" Lane asked.

"Okay." Eva stuffed her feet into shoes and grabbed a ball cap. "Comin'?" She looked at Aidan.

Lane backed down the stairs and waited.

Aidan opened the door, sat down on the steps and

put on a pair of boots. She stood to hold the door open for Eva.

A hummingbird swooped in, hovered, and stuck its beak into the nectar of one of the fuchsia's blossoms. Lane, Aidan, and Eva watched until the bird zipped away.

Eva led the way past the car and along a path. They walked up a rise. At the crest, the downtown towers could be seen through the morning haze. "City'll be here pretty soon."

"I'm sorry," Lane said.

Eva turned to him.

Lane felt a tightness in his chest making it difficult to form the words. "I saw the box of shells and the rifle bolt in your kitchen cupboard. I put it all together too late. Norm should never have been shot."

Eva looked back toward the city. "You tried to stop it."

Aidan stood beside her and put her arm through Eva's.

"I was too late," Lane said.

"Stood out in the open and tried to stop it," Eva said.

Lane shook his head. He looked past the women to the silhouettes of city buildings in the distance. There was no denying the city was creeping this way.

"Like I said before. We're here. You're here. None of us have got anywhere else to go. Gotta learn to live with each other. It took a while, but the boys at the blockade are beginning to understand." Eva turned to Lane. "And, you came to our sweat. Then you came to the blockade with coffee instead of soldiers. That's a start."

"You didn't judge me," Lane said.

"Look at how European religion treated some of us in the residential schools. Judgin's the wrong way to go." Eva almost maintained her impassive expression.

Lane thought, *That's always been the problem: judgement.*

"Norm's funeral is tomorrow at ten. You and Harper be there?" Eva asked.

"I'll be there. Harper's wife is ..." *How do I say this?* Lane thought.

Eva waited.

Aidan watched him with curious expectation.

"She just had a baby. She's afraid of what might happen to Harper," Lane said.

"Oh." Eva studied Lane's face. "You still have to find those other two, don't you?"

"Yes." Lane looked at his feet.

"Those bastards killed Alex," Aidan said.

Eva looked at Aidan, then spoke to Lane. "Hatred eats us up from the inside. Been tryin' to figure out where Norm might have put those two boys. Could be anywhere." Eva looked west to where the prairies rolled up to the foothills and the mountains.

"We could be looking forever," Lane said.

"Harper can bring his family if he likes. And you too. Small funerals are sad. Nothing else besides that for you to be worried about. Nobody's gonna hurt you. People been talkin' about you and how you brought coffee to the barricade. How you waited and listened. How you laid your gun down. Lot of the people around here have respect for you now," Eva said.

Aidan nodded without smiling.

ch*a*pter 21

Lane and Harper stood with their backs to the wall at the rear of the church. It was half the size of a double-wide mobile home. The building was surrounded by mature trees with trunks too wide to embrace. The inside of the church was tilted back to front. It seemed as if the building had been deposited there by a flood.

Two men rolled Norm's coffin up to the front of the church. The width of the aisle wouldn't have allowed for pallbearers. Eva and Aidan followed the coffin. They sat in two folding chairs across from Norm's closed coffin.

Lane said, "The place is packed."

Harper looked out the window at those peering inside.

Eva stood up and turned. She looked at the people outside. She pointed at the windows. "Open 'em up so everybody can hear."

Five minutes later, the minister gave a short sermon, then said, "Eva Starchild?"

Eva stood.

Complete silence fell over the inside and outside of the church.

"My best memory of Norm was him handing a log to Bruce." Eva nodded at a man who nodded back at her. The man stood next to Lane. "Bruce and Norm were cutting some deadfall near the river. Norm handed the wood over a barbed-wire fence to Bruce. Bruce then piled the pieces in the back of his old Ford pickup. You know, the truck that finally died last year. Anyway, Norm was gently handing those logs over the fence. Bruce's knees nearly buckled from the weight of each log."

Lane looked at Bruce, who stood over six feet and crossed his thick arms across his chest. Bruce smiled at the memory.

"Norm was strong and gentle. He watched over Alex, Aidan, and me. He carried a weight that many of us would have found too heavy." Eva looked around the church, at the faces watching her. She looked at Lane and Harper.

"There's been some talk of revenge over the way Norm died." Eva looked at a couple of young men near the window who developed a sudden interest in their shoes. "The time for revenge is over. Revenge would have put Norm in a cage. He would have gone crazy in a cage. Alex died. Four boys died." She looked at the coffin. "Too many people have died for no good reason. Everyone here will keep an eye out so we can all be safe."

Eva sat down.

"We'll meet at the cemetery," the minister said.

Norm's coffin was rolled down the aisle.

Lane and Harper, waiting until everyone left, followed.

In the car, they trailed the procession of cars and the cloud of dust.

"How's Erinn?" Lane asked.

"Better. She told me to come. Now she's apologizing for her meltdown." Harper frowned.

"Arthur went over to visit her this morning. He said he knows how she feels. Maybe she'll feel better after they talk." Lane watched the cars stop. Their doors opened.

A group of six men carried the coffin to the open grave.

Harper parked. When they opened their doors, they could hear chanting and the sound of a drum. Lane saw eight men around a drum singing for Norm. Harper and Lane walked up the slope. The mountain peaks gradually revealed their massive shoulders as the detectives reached the top of the hill.

Eva and Aidan walked toward Lane and Harper after Norm was buried beside his mother.

Eva asked, "Any idea where those other boys are?"

Aidan looked away at the mountains.

Lane turned to Harper.

"When can we come and visit your place?" Harper asked.

Aidan turned to them. "You think the bodies are there?"

"It's a possibility," Lane said.

"Wouldn't we know about it, then?" Aidan's voice was laced with sarcasm.

Lane watched as Eva touched Aidan's arm. She lowered her eyes.

Eva looked at Harper. "What's the matter?"

Harper looked back at her. "My wife is afraid. We just had a daughter, and she's afraid of raising Jessica on her own."

Eva smiled. "The only thing you have to worry

about is my muffins. Come by tomorrow. Right now, we got people coming over to the house. You comin'?"

Lane thought, *I won't know a soul.* He looked at Harper, who looked as afraid as he felt. "Can we come by tomorrow morning?"

Eva smirked. "Up to you. What do you need?"

"A backhoe," Harper said.

"I'll call Judith. She'll be there in the morning." Eva walked away.

Lane watched as two men with shovels began to scoop earth into Norm's grave. Somehow, Eva's words at the church had eased his sense of guilt.

SATURDAY, JULY 20

ch*a*pter 22

Kuldeep asked, "The usual?"

Lane looked at Christine, who stood next to Kuldeep behind the counter. He smiled. "Yes, please."

Christine and Kuldeep smiled back.

"Hi Christine." Harper stood behind Lane.

"Good morning." Christine stood a head taller than Kuldeep.

"You two know each other?" Kuldeep moved to the espresso machine.

"That's my uncle and his friend." Christine studied Kuldeep's moves as she prepared the espresso machine.

"You want to make these two coffees, then?" Kuldeep asked.

"Sure." Christine sounded like her confidence might evaporate with the steam.

Kuldeep put a hand on Christine's shoulder. "No problem."

Lane pulled out twenty dollars. Kuldeep took the bill, handed him his change. He dropped the change in the tip jar.

"We'll bring those out to you," Kuldeep said.

Lane and Harper sat down.

"Christine's first day?" Harper asked.

"Started yesterday." Lane watched the top of Christine's head. It was all that was visible behind the espresso machine.

"How's Erinn doing?" Lane asked.

"She slept last night. Jessica slept though the night. Glenn's home today, and he'll keep an eye on things. He's been amazing." Harper looked out the window. "What time will Fibre be at Eva's?"

"He said eleven." Lane watched as Christine brought their coffees over. Her eyes went from one cup to the next intent on not spilling.

"Thanks," Harper and Lane said in unison as she set the cups down.

"Hope they're the way you like them." She waited for them to take the first sip.

Lane picked up the cup and took a sip. *Wow! I'm going to be awake for two days after this!* he thought. "Tastes great!"

Harper nodded. "Mine too!"

Christine smiled and went back behind the counter.

"How come Christine is always expecting the worst?" Harper asked.

Lane's phone rang. He flipped it open. "Hello?"

"Some woman named Eva is telling you to get out to her place. The backhoe is waiting and you're late," the officer said.

"Thanks." Lane closed the phone. "We've got to go." He stood up and went to get lids for their coffees. "See you later." He lifted his cup to Kuldeep and Christine.

When they got outside, Harper asked, "What's up?"

"The backhoe is waiting. We're late."

"Everybody knows Judith starts at seven in the morning." Eva leaned on a shovel next to the yellow backhoe. Aidan stood closer to the honeysuckle in the shade of the evergreens.

Judith leaned out the window. She wore pink earrings and a white dirt-stained ball cap with a silver bow stuck on the top. Her tank top was white and sparkling. One breast hung lower than the other. "Where do I start?" She held up a deerskin-gloved hand.

Lane looked at Harper.

"At the evergreens." Harper pointed south.

"Nobody's diggin' up Alex's trees." Eva stood between them and the backhoe.

Aidan moved over next to Eva.

"I thought we might dig a trench behind those two." Harper smiled and pointed at two trees. One had more new growth at the tips of the branches than its neighbours. Two trees over was an evergreen freshly planted and staked to the earth. "That way we could find out what's underneath without harming the trees."

Eva considered this for a minute. She turned to Judith.

Judith studied Eva's expression. "I can do it. It won't hurt the trees. Besides, this is your place. I listen to you, Eva."

Eva nodded.

Aidan asked, "Why the trees?"

Harper said, "It looks like one has been fertilized. The others haven't."

Eva and Aidan looked at the trees. One was taller than the one planted a year before. They looked at each other, considering what this might mean.

"Norm said Alex looked for trees of a specific height before he planted them, and Norm was very careful to respect Alex's wishes. We'd like to see what's under those two trees and why one is growing faster than the others." Harper waited for a response.

"I'll stop Judith if it looks like the trees will be harmed," Eva said.

"Your land," Lane said.

With a nod from Eva, Judith engaged the tractor's starter. Its diesel engine clattered to life. A gout of black smoke puffed from its exhaust. They followed the backhoe as it bounced around to the far side of the trees.

As Judith braced the backhoe with its hydraulic wings, Eva held out her hand. "Give me your jackets and ties."

Lane and Harper did as they were told. Eva handed Lane a shovel. "Do what Judith says. I'll go make some coffee."

Lane leaned with his hands and chin on the shovel handle.

Aidan smiled at him and climbed into the cab with Judith. Harper studied the placement of the machine.

Judith turned the seat around to face backwards. Her hands danced over the hydraulic levers. The backhoe reached out to shave away the top layer of earth. Under Judith's guidance, the machine moved with confidence and grace.

Aidan jumped down and walked over to Harper. "How deep do you want her to go?"

Harper shrugged. "How deep would Norm make the hole before planting a tree?"

Aidan climbed back up into the cab and passed the message on to Judith. She nodded.

Eva arrived with coffee after Judith had dug a trench two metres deep and five metres long.

They sat down in the shade for coffee and muffins after Judith shut the backhoe down.

Judith said, "I'm gonna dig down a bit more and then start shaving dirt from the side nearest the trees. You guys keep your eyes open just in case I hit a root."

"A forensics team should be here soon." Harper took a muffin in one hand and sipped at the coffee in the other.

Aidan and Judith looked at Eva.

Eva sat cross-legged, looked at the trees, and said nothing.

After the break, Judith and Aidan climbed back into the cab.

Eva, Harper, and Lane watched as Judith shaved a layer of soil and clay from the side of the trench. She inched gradually, artfully closer to the trees. Aidan climbed down from the machine to watch from the far end of the trench.

A hummingbird hovered within a hand's length of Lane's nose. A translucent tongue slipped out. The tongue was nearly as long as the beak. Lane thought, *It's almost long enough to touch the tip of my nose.* He could feel the gentle frenzy of its wings. Hear the whirring of its muscles. The hummingbird was there for nearly half a minute, studying him as he studied it. The bird flew off to Lane's left. He memorized its image and the sensations it took with it. "Cool."

Aidan moved up beside Lane.

Lane said, "You had Alex do a hummingbird dance."

"Alex used to study them so he could imitate their moves at powwows. He did some research and found out the ones who travelled this far north are called Rufous hummingbirds. When a group of them fought over the honeysuckle, he'd laugh and say they were acting like people. Thought it was a huge joke. Hummingbirds fighting over one honeysuckle flower when there were plenty to go around. And then he thought it was even funnier because giving all hummingbirds one name was crazy. He thought of them more as individuals. He said when the Europeans got here they messed up everything. Decided they had the right to own land. Invented names for every little thing. He said the hummingbirds were just like the people who picked out a spot and then tried to push everyone else away from it." She waited for a minute, deep in thought. "That hummer, it stopped to take a look at you. That hasn't happened since Alex was alive. He thought they were trying to communicate somehow, but the gap between people and birds had become too wide. I always thought it was funny that the beauty of the hummingbirds could remind him of how badly humans treat one another."

"You know, I've never seen a hummingbird up close before." Lane glanced at Aidan, who stared at him.

"If you read what the experts write in books, hummingbirds are not even supposed to stay here all summer. They're supposed to move on. Eva says that hummingbirds have been coming here for the summer as long as she has. And there've been more hummers the last few years. Even the birds around here don't act the way they're supposed to. Eva's personality must be rubbing off on the birds too." Aidan sipped at her coffee.

"I guess that's why you belong at Eva's." Lane smiled.

Aidan's eyes narrowed, then widened as she smiled at Lane's joke.

Lane spotted a pair of white-covered boots standing at the edge of the hole. He looked up into the face of Dr. Fibre in his bunny suit.

Judith stopped digging and the engine idled.

"Dr. Colin Weaver," Fibre introduced himself to Eva. He bowed.

Judith said, "For Christ's sake, she's First Nations, not Asian!"

"Lookin' for rabbits?" Eva asked.

Aidan began to laugh. Pretty soon, Fibre was the only one not laughing.

Judith got back to work.

Five minutes later, she was still skimming the wall of the trench. At the depth of about a metre-and-a-half, the heel and sole of a cowboy boot stuck out of the earth.

Harper waved his arms in the air. Judith lifted the bucket out of the way. Fibre climbed into the hole. He used a trowel to scoop earth away from above and below the boot.

The stink of decomposing flesh caught at the back of Lane's throat. He looked at the others, who had gathered around the edge of the trench.

Eva shook her head.

Fibre stopped and looked up at them. "I'm going to need my team." He looked at Aidan, who had her hand over her mouth and nose. "I'll get some masks."

"How long's Uncle Lane been in the shower?" Matt asked.

Arthur wiped sweat from his forehead. At this time of the day, the sun baked the deck. He opened the lid of the barbecue.

"Smells good." Christine sat in a lawn chair in a tiny corner of shade, sipping a pop.

"Lane doesn't …" Arthur turned the chicken breasts over and basted them with a mixture of ginger, sesame oil, honey, and soy sauce.

"Doesn't what?" Matt leaned back and closed his eyes.

"… smell good. They found two bodies today. Every time this happens he throws his clothes in the wash and heads for the shower. He can't seem to get the stench off of his skin or out of his mind." Arthur closed the lid of the barbecue.

"This is nothing like I expected," Christine said.

Arthur sat down next to Christine. He saw that her skin was getting darker from time spent in the sun. He reached down and petted Roz who lay on her side under his chair. "What's nothing like you expected?"

"You and Uncle Lane. This house." Christine looked nervously at Matt, who'd opened his eyes.

"The way other people in the family talked about you I thought …" Christine hesitated.

Arthur looked at her. "Well?"

Matt said, "I didn't know what to expect, either. What I was told and what it is like, well, they're two different things."

"That's right. It's not at all like I was told it would be." Christine smiled at Matt.

Arthur looked puzzled.

"We like it here, is all we're trying to say." Matt shifted his weight.

Arthur smiled and rubbed Roz's belly.

SUNDAY, JULY 21

ch*a*pter 23

"Ryan Dudley's identity is confirmed. They found his ID. The body has already been removed. It was the first one we found. Fibre just wants to be absolutely sure, so the dental records are being checked." Harper looked down into the hole behind the evergreens. Fibre's crew was working steadily with another set of remains.

Lane asked, "Tyler McNally?"

"Probably, but it will take a while to confirm. This one will definitely require dental records." Harper stepped away from the hole. "A hole was found in Dudley's skull. It was near the ear. The autopsy will reveal whether or not it's a bullet wound. By the size and shape, it's likely to be a twenty-two round."

Eva walked up and stood beside them. "The other guy?"

"Yes." Lane spotted the dark circles under Eva's eyes. "No sleep?"

"Nope." Eva looked from the hole to the trees. "Norm thought he had to protect us."

"Makes you wonder," Lane said.

Eva waited for Lane to explain.

Harper asked, "What?"

"Norm was eight or nine up here." Lane tapped the side of his skull. "He had more than enough smarts to fool us all for more than a year."

"I wondered why he wouldn't let us help plant the trees." Eva looked west toward Norm's house.

"When I first met him, he chatted about hunting. I didn't realize he was also hunting the guys who killed Alex," Harper said.

"Did Aidan know?" Lane asked.

"Nope." Eva kept her eyes on Lane when she answered.

"Who else could he have told?" Harper asked.

"If he told anyone else, I would've heard about it," Eva said.

It was still too hot inside the house at nine o'clock, so the four of them sat on the deck and sipped drinks.

Ice clinked against glass. The sky above the mountains was painted yellow and orange. Roz lay under Matt's chair.

"How's the job going?" Arthur asked.

"Fine." Christine chuckled. "Just never saw myself making money in a coffee shop. There wasn't much coffee in Paradise." She looked down at Roz.

"I applied at the golf course," Matt said.

Lane smiled at him. "What kind of work?"

"I wanted to drive the beer cart, but they said I had to wait until I was eighteen. They do have some openings for greenskeepers." Matt aimed his chin in Christine's direction.

Lane turned to his niece. "Christine?"

Christine turned toward him.

"Arthur and I were wondering about your plans." Lane sat straighter in his chair.

"You want me to move out, don't you?" Christine began to stand.

"No! Will you stop that? We wondered if you were going back to school in the fall. We hoped you'd consider staying, actually."

Arthur looked at Lane.

Lane stumbled along. "We thought you might want to go to university or college?"

"We weren't allowed," Christine said.

"Weren't allowed to what?" Matt asked.

"Women in Paradise weren't supposed to go to school past grade ten." She looked back and forth between Lane and Arthur.

"Do you want to go to school and do you want to live here?" Lane asked.

"Yes," Matt said. "Of course she does."

Christine looked past them to the end of the deck where honeysuckle grew out of pots and a fuchsia plant hung from a hook on the fence. "What is that?"

Lane turned his head to see a hummingbird with its beak deep into a white honeysuckle bloom. There was a blur of green wings, some red at the bird's throat. It reversed and, with impossible speed, was gone.

"Cool," Matt said.

Lane thought, *She hasn't answered the question.*

*a*cknowledgements

Bruce, for caring for us all of these years, and for early detection, thank you.

Justine, Colin, Don, Barry, and Holly, thanks for answering odd questions.

Doug, Bob, Nicki, and Luke, thanks for the skilled editing of scenes.

MaryAnne and Jim, thanks for the elephant and hummingbirds.

Amber, Ruth, Lou, Katherine, Alice, Diane, Doug, Michael, Tiffany, and Jennifer, thanks for all that you do.

For many kindnesses, thank you Herb, Anthony Bidulka, and Wayne Gunn.

Thank you, Lambda Literary Awards.

Thanks to creative writers at Nickle, Bowness, Lord Beaverbrook, Alternative, Forest Lawn, and Queen Elizabeth.

Thank you, Sharon, Ben, Karma, Luke, and Indiana— the family.

Find out how it all began! Pick up the first two Detective Lane mysteries from your local bookseller.

The Lucky Elephant Restaurant, winner of the 2007 Lambda Literary Award for Gay Mystery
Detective Lane is back, tracking trouble on the streets of Calgary with his sharp-eyed partner Harper in tow. The duo must find the missing daughter of local radio celebrity Bobbie Reddie before it's too late. But is Bobbie as saintly as her fans believe? Lane must uncover the truth, or this time the danger will hit much closer to home.

Queen's Park
After a brutal attack on his young nephew, ex-mayor Bob Swatzky has disappeared with 13 million dollars worth of taxpayers' money. Is he simply on the run with the cash, or is it something more sinister? A zany cast of characters lead Detective Lane on a thrilling romp through the streets of Calgary as he tries to uncover the truth before someone ends up visiting Queen's Park cemetery ... permanently.

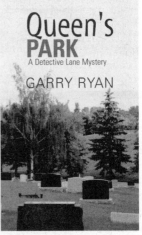

Garry Ryan was born and raised in Calgary, Alberta, where he lives today. He received a B.Ed. and a Diploma in Educational Psychology from the University of Calgary, and now teaches junior high and high school students. His first Detective Lane mystery, *Queen's Park*, sprung from a desire to write a mystery with an emphasis on the rich diversity and unique locations of his hometown. *The Lucky Elephant Restaurant* is the second title in his Detective Lane Mystery Series and winner of the 2007 Lambda Literary Award for Gay Mystery.